Death and the Chaste Apprentice

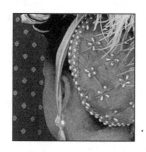

Death and the Chaste Apprentice

Robert Barnard

All the characters and events portrayed in this work are fictitious.

DEATH AND THE CHASTE APPRENTICE

A Felony & Mayhem mystery

PRINTING HISTORY
First UK edition (Collins Crime Club): 1989
First U.S. edition (Charles Scribner's Sons): 1989
Felony & Mayhem edition: 2007
Reprinted by permission of Scribner, an imprint
of Simon & Schuster, Inc.

ISBN-10: 1-933397-63-2
ISBN-13: 978-1-933397-63-4

Manufactured in the United States of America

NOTE

The extracts from the supposed *The Chaste Apprentice of Bowe* are in fact taken from *A Trick to Catch the Old One*, *'Tis Pity She's a Whore*, and other plays of the Elizabethan and Jacobean period. So don't blame me.

Contents

The icon above says you're holding a copy of a book in the Felony & Mayhem "British" category. These books are set in or around the UK, and feature the highly literate, often witty prose that fans of British mystery demand. If you enjoy this book, you may well like other "British" titles from Felony & Mayhem Press, including:

The Killings at Badger's Drift, by Caroline Graham
Death of a Hollow Man, by Caroline Graham
Murder at Madingley Grange, by Caroline Graham
Death on the High C's, by Robert Barnard
Out of the Blackout, by Robert Barnard
Death in the Garden, by Elizabeth Ironside
The Accomplice, by Elizabeth Ironside
Dupe, by Liza Cody
King and Joker, by Peter Dickinson
Death in the Morning, by Sheila Radley
Death of a Dormouse, by Reginald Hill

For more about these books, and other Felony & Mayhem titles, or to place an order, please visit our website at:

www.FelonyAndMayhem.com

or contact us at:

Felony and Mayhem Press
156 Waverly Place
New York, NY 10014

Death and the Chaste Apprentice

Chapter 1

THE SARACEN'S HEAD

"Mad as a hatter," said Gillian Soames complacently, striding up the road from the underground towards Ketterick High Street. "Stark raving bonkers. Up the wall. Round the twist to an unprecedented degree."

Peter Fortnum, legging it beside her through the town, was surprised to see on her face an expression of quite sunny anticipation. After all, she was talking about Jason Thark, the producer-director of the play in which they both were to appear. The two had met on the underground, having previously done no more than swap words when they were in different productions at the Sheffield Crucible. Thus they were still in the earliest stages of mutual discovery.

Peter Fortnum was slim, fresh, and twenty-three. Gillian Soames was rather plain, beginning to be dumpy, and was a stage veteran of eight years in small parts. She had had her share of theatrical disasters and had gone on from them to other disasters or to the occasional minor triumph. She knew that this was a festival production, which would run its allotted course of twelve performances and never be heard of again, quite irrespective of the merits or otherwise of the production. Peter Fortnum was a nice lad, she was saying to herself, but you could spot the wetness behind his ears: He still believed that stardom might be just around the corner. Gillian knew that hard work was.

"So be prepared to swallow your artistic conscience," she added darkly.

"He's got a tremendous reputation," Peter ventured.

"Oh—reputation!"

Gillian's tone seemed to contain a limitless scorn for drama critics. Thus did Lady Bracknell dismiss cloakrooms at railway stations. Peter wondered whether Gillian wasn't, perhaps, a Lady Bracknell in waiting. But if she meant that directors' reputations were gained over the bodies of actors who knew better, then Peter could go along with that.

"People do say he does interesting things," he amended.

"The sort of director who gets that said about him," said Gillian, still with the same unruffled composure, "is the kind to run a mile from. What does it usually mean? If the play cries out for a simple, direct approach, he decks it out with moving sets, Wurlitzer organs, and so many spots it looks like the Battle of Britain. And if the play is weak and needs a bit of gingering up, he puts the characters in body stockings and sets it in the Gobi Desert. That sort of director's motto is 'Don't notice the play; notice *me!*'"

"Well, he can't play about much with an Elizabethan stage," Peter pointed out.

"That's true," conceded Gillian with all the reluctance of the born prophet of doom. "At least you wouldn't have *thought* he could. The critics will come down on him if he tries any modern tricksiness, that's for sure. Still—"

She stopped short in her stride as she and Peter noticed simultaneously a poster for the play in an arty little bookshop. They peered into the window, and Peter read out the title with a reverence the play hardly warranted:

THE CHASTE APPRENTICE OF BOWE

The poster was done in the form of a playbill—of the Restoration rather than any conceivable Elizabethan type. Peter's and Gillian's heads slowly dipped down as they read through the list of the players' names. There at the bottom they were: Peter Fortnum and Gillian Soames.

"At least we got on," said Peter.

"Which is more than the author did."

"It was published anonymously."

"Nobody willing to own up," said Gillian cheerily. "It does come rather into the 'justly neglected' category, doesn't it?" They resumed their lithe stride in the direction of the High Street. "Actually, I'd do a walk-on part in the worst play of Robert Greene just for the pleasure of working at the Saracen."

"It must be fabulous," agreed Peter. "Like getting back to one's roots—starting again at the beginnings of drama."

"Something like that," agreed Gillian, who distrusted enthusiasm.

"And actually staying there, too! I thought we'd be shunted off to some crummy bed-and-breakfast dive, with rooms at the Saracen reserved for the stars."

"That's not how they do things at Ketterick. The

theory is that there *are* no stars—which is bullshit, but useful bullshit. Of course, a lot of the names have flats or houses in London, anyway. Some of the rest prefer to take theatrical digs. I've got a poky room in north London which I've loaned to a friend for the summer."

"And I'm living out of a suitcase at the moment. I could have got cheaper digs, but just the idea of staying at the place..."

"Precisely. It has an aura. And at the Saracen's Head somebodies and nobodies rub shoulders and swap pints. That's something Arthur has insisted on from—Oh!"

"What?"

"Dear old Arthur. The landlord of the Saracen. I'd forgotten for a moment that he'd died."

"Was he nice?"

"The dearest old man. And one of the masterminds behind the festival. He treated everyone alike, from Hamlet to Second Gent. I suppose the place must have been sold or something. Anyway, we'll soon see."

They turned a corner into a wide but not too busy street, and Giilian pointed histrionically. "There it is," she said.

As if they had but one mind, they set down their cases and gazed.

Even from a distance, viewed through the clutter and bustle of an outer-London suburb, the Saracen's Head looked like something special, something rather out of the run of old English inns. You noticed first its long frontage, which straddled a huge pair of gates. Through these, coaches had once rumbled to disgorge their passengers in the great yard beyond, for Ketterick had been a stopping-place between the north and Dover for fast coaches that had shunned the center of London. As you moved closer, you noticed that, apart from plaster over the half-timbering, it had been neither renovated nor tarted up, but had been left blessedly alone. The Saracen's Head had benefited over the centuries from a family of landlords who were quite remarkably slothful, men who could just about bring themselves to pull a pint but not much more. One of them, it is true, had in the mid-eighteenth century attempted something in the way of modernization, but fortunately he had died, and in his son the family inertia had reasserted itself. In the nineteenth century the railway had removed its principal function, and in the twentieth century hideous shopping precincts and mails had diverted a lot of traffic from Ketterick High Street. The Saracen's Head had slumbered on until it was rediscovered by architectural and theatrical historians in our own century. The sleeping princess had been re-awakened by the kiss of the Ketterick Arts Festival.

As Peter and Gillian approached, past the modern facades of video shops and Marks and Spencers, the great gates at the center of the facade were pushed open.

"Half past five," said Gillian, licking her lips with satisfaction. "Opening time."

Peter, seeing it for the first time, took in the details of the frontage as they stood on the other side of the road, waiting to cross. It was an untidy, welcoming facade. To the left of the great gates were the Massinger Bar and the Webster Bar. To the right, Reception and the Shakespeare Bar.

"The Shakespeare Bar's ours," said Gillian authoritatively. "Not that the festival ever does Shakespeare."

"No, we're stuck with *The Chaste Apprentice of Bowe.*"

"Anyway, they were just the Toby Bar, the Snug, and so on until the festival started. Even dear old Arthur wasn't averse to capitalizing."

They crossed the road, and from an unspoken wish they walked straight through the massive gates and into the great courtyard. Here they stopped, and Peter looked around with reverence at the open space within which they would be playing. Here the Lord Admiral's Men and the Lord Chamberlain's Men had played when forced from London's South bank by the plague or the hostility of City aldermen. The Saracen was, at ground-floor level, the usual array of bars, dining rooms and kitchens, and the other inevitable offices of a large hotel. But at first- and second-floor level, on three of its four sides, it had kept the balconies from which the better class of Ketterick spectators had watched the entertainments provided by the traveling players. On the fourth side, the inn's proprietor of the eighteenth century, in that brief and regrettable spurt of energy, had bricked in the balconies and enlarged the bedrooms behind. Enough remained, with the row upon row of seats in the great courtyard itself, to provide sizable audiences for the Elizabethan and Jacobean revivals that were the staple of the Ketterick Arts Festival.

Even as they stood, silent, antennae a-twitch to get the feel of the place, a couple of late workmen came out with two more sections of the stage. They began fixing them on to the section already set up, which was beginning to project out from the kitchens at the far side of the courtyard to form an apron stage. It was on this bare platform that the festival company had performed *The Devil's an*

Ass, The Faire Seducer, The Roaring Girls of Cheapside, and other minor masterpieces of our drama. It was on this platform that Peter and Gillian would perform lesser roles in *The Chaste Apprentice of Bowe.*

"Our stage," said Gillian with satisfaction in her voice, and reverence too. "You're right. It's difficult to see what Jason Thark can do to bugger *that* up."

They watched the workmen and the embryonic stage, silent and companionable, united in some powerful but indefinable respect for their own art and its beginnings. Their mood was brutally shattered by an interruption.

"Would you be the operatic lady and gentleman?"

The voice had an Australian twang, and when they turned, they saw a bulky presence, now running to fat— an ex-rugby football player, perhaps, or the regiment's champion middleweight boxer. He was dressed in a suit of good cloth but baggy proportions, was balding, and his eyes were watery, shifting, and ill focused. But what was most immediately off-putting was his manner, which was unpleasingly ingratiating, yet oddly combined with something cunning, something almost threatening. He oozed up to them, it was true, but his manner had as its subtext something of the bully, as if he were itching to get them under his thumb.

"I'm Des Capper, the landlord," he said.

"Oh." Gillian Soames hardly bothered to keep the layers of meaning out of her voice. After a moment's hesitation she shook his hand because she could hardly avoid it. She did it in a manner that suggested she had already made up her mind he was a lousy replacement for dear old Arthur. "No, we're not the operatic lady and gentleman. We're both in *The Chaste Apprentice.*"

Des Capper's face fell, and his manner lost several degrees of ingratiation.

"Oh. Suppose I should have known. The operatic people tend to come larger, don't they? It's the lung capacity that does it, you know— It's the lung capacity that makes or breaks a singer. You must be Miss Soames and Mr. Fortnum, then?"

"That's right."

"Playing Alison Greatheart and Peter Patterwit."

"Right."

"Most of the principals have been here a week or more."

"The leads always come early. We are not leads."

"Well, I'm sure you'll make something very nice of your respective roles," said Des Capper, leading the way towards Reception and making no move to help Gillian with her suitcase. "It's not the size of the role that counts, you know. A good actor can make a marvelous thing out of a juicy little part. I've seen it happen."

"We know," muttered Gillian. "We *are* actors."

"Just so long as you speak up and speak out," Des went on, disregarding her. "You can't get away with mumbling on this stage, oh, dear me, no."

"I have appeared in five of the eight productions here," said Gillian, acid-sweetly.

"Then you'll bear me out when I say speak up and speak out. The way some of these young actors produce their voices must have dear old Sir John Gielgud turning in his grave."

"He's still alive."

"That makes it worse. Personally I think it's all part of your mental approach to the part." Des, ensconced behind the reception desk, absently shoved little cards in front of them to sign as he continued to lecture them on their profession. "Have you tried yoga? There's many actors that do. I've got a terrific book of yoga exercises I could loan you. Incredible. They've changed my life, I can tell you... What? Room numbers? Oh, yes. Have you filled in the cards? Fine. You're 227, Miss Soames, and you're 234, Mr. Fortnum. Close without being adjacent." He leered. "Can you find your own way? You should never pick up a heavy case like that, young man. You can do terrible damage to your dorsals that way. I've known people ruined by it, and an actor ought to be specially careful." He came round from behind the desk and put himself in a posture of demonstration. "What you should do is *bend* the knees slightly, go *down* to it, then lift it smoothly like *this*...Got it? Don't mind me telling you, do you?"

By now the nature of the new landlord of the Saracen's Head needed no further defining in either of their minds. He was that most loathsome of God's creations, the Australian know-all. They both gave him smiles that scarcely rose to the level of the perfunctory and set off in the direction of their rooms.

Or roughly speaking in the direction of their rooms. The old inn was a maze of corridors, obscure passageways that ended in blank walls, inexplicable open areas that must once have served a purpose but which now seemed merely to be dumping places for unwanted pieces of furniture. The inn was innocent of lifts, which in any case would have been of limited use: The Saracen's sprawl was not vertical but horizontal. Discreet wooden arrows pointed in the direction of room numbers, which were allocated with the same beautiful lack of logic or pattern as the general layout of the place.

"I love it," said Gillian as they toiled back along a

passage that had led merely to a laundry cupboard. "Do you know, I've stayed here five seasons, and I still haven't fathomed it. And I still expect to hear Tom Jones and one of his doxies from one of the bedrooms."

But it was not Tom Jones that they heard.

"And if you upstage me again at the end of Act One, by God I'll have your guts for garters."

They were in one of those inexplicable open spaces, and the voice came from the bedroom or suite that led off from it. It was a male voice that was clearly accustomed to making itself heard in large spaces—a traditional theater voice. Gillian held up a finger and—still holding their cases, fearing they might have to make a hurried exit—they stood listening with the telling stillness of stage actors.

"Carston Galloway," whispered Gillian.

"I did not upstage you. You seem not to want to acknowledge that there *is* anyone else onstage."

"I am perfectly willing to cooperate with real company players. They wouldn't try to ruin each other's performances."

"Oh God, don't talk to me about your performance. Talk to your little backstage drab about that."

"Darling Clarissa," whispered Gillian.

"I suppose that *swoop* to the front was something you arranged with dear Jason in bed?"

"Darling, we have *quite* other things to think about when we are in bed."

"Crap. Sex may be important to you—God knows, I've reason enough to know that it is—but nothing is more important to you than the shoddy little theatrical victories you arrange for yourself. So don't feed me that shit about sex being all in all."

"I love your exquisitely modulated guttersnipe language."

The Galloways were doing their daily exercises. They were famous in theatrical circles for the fearlessly open way in which they conducted their sex lives. The odd thing was that for all their openness and honesty, their emotional lives were just as great a mess as if they had been secret about it.

"I've always been so *sorry* for you," said Clarissa in a lethal purr. "There are so few female directors. And the ones there are direct practically nothing but all-female plays. It does frustrate your instinct to pay back in kind. So you have to content yourself with ingenues and assistant stage managers...nobodies. Still, I suppose they renew your youth, which heaven knows has lasted longer than most people's youth."

"My God! Coming from you..."

Gillian shook her head at Peter Fortnum, and together they stole down the corridor. A floorboard creaked under them, as floorboards could be relied upon to do at the Saracen when one was trying to be circumspect. It was unlikely that the Galloways in full flood would notice or care.

"Par for the course," said Gillian when they were out of earshot. "We can expect a feast of that in the next week or two. Ever worked with them before?"

"No," admitted Peter. "I've mostly been in pretty experimental stuff. Disused warehouses and upstairs rooms in pubs. That's not really their line, is it?"

"Oh, dear me, no. The thought of Clarissa in a Hackney pub is practically lèse majesté. Revivals of *Lady Windermere* or *The School for Scandal*—all powdered wigs and rustling taffeta—that's the Galloways' line. I believe Rattigan was about to write something for them when he died, and they certainly created some minor roles in late Coward. They're a practically extinct theatrical breed."

"The giant egos?"

"Well, that particular form of giant ego. Nowadays it takes different forms. The day giant egos are extinct in the theater we may as well all shut up shop and go home…Good Lord, we're here. Do you think we'll ever find our way here again—or find our way out, for that matter?"

They put their keys in their doors and swung them open. Each discovered they were in unlovely little boxes clearly furnished with castoffs from other rooms.

"It's all right," said Peter cheerfully. "I never expected anything better."

"It's *not* how dear old Arthur used to organize things. All the actors were given good rooms. Still, at least we've got a view of the courtyard and the stage."

They went to the window of Gillian's room. At the far end of the courtyard the stage was a little further towards completion—that great projecting space that would so cruelly expose any faults in their techniques, any immaturities or imperfections. Peter drew his eyes away, almost in fear. Down in the front part of the courtyard Des Capper was oozing forward again, this time to welcome a woman and two men, who had been disgorged from a taxi, and had come in to view the great space.

"Probably the operatic lady and gentleman," said Peter. "And if so, they're *not* large."

"Have you ever known that sort of blowhard to get things right?" Gillian asked bitterly. "Is that young one Indian? He looks rather plump, an incipient fatty. No doubt Des Capper will put that down to his lung capacity. Actually the woman looks decidedly presentable. I say— just look at Des! Look at the way he's fawning and scraping! It's a fair bet they're the stars of whatever it is, isn't it? Isn't he odious? Stomach-turning! Look, he's even rubbing his hands. He's one of the most ghastly men I've met."

"He doesn't seem much of a replacement for your Arthur," agreed Peter. "I wonder why they appointed him."

"Appointed? I thought he must have bought the place or something."

"Didn't you see the plaque outside? It said the Saracen was one of the Beaumont chain of hotels. He called himself the landlord, but he must be some kind of manager."

"Really? Well, someone who's appointed can be sacked. The festival committee ought to do something about it. There must be some way he can be got rid of."

She said it casually. Others in the course of the next week or two were to say or think the same thing with more vehement emphasis.

Chapter 2

THE SHAKESPEARE BAR

Gillian and. Peter went out for their meal that evening. There was a little bistro called The Relief of Mafeking, Gillian said, where you could get a wholesome nosh-up for £2.95. In fact, they found the price had gone up way beyond the rate of inflation, as it did with most good things once they caught on, but it was a satisfactory bargain all the same. Even actors in work—and Peter was only intermittently so—had to watch their pennies.

"I never eat at the Saracen before I've got my first paycheck," Gillian explained over the chicken casserole, "and then only every three or four days. It's very pricey, though the food is marvelous," She added darkly: "Mind you, it's probably shark meat and kangaroo steaks nowadays."

She did not actually sing "Change and decay in all around I see," but the dust of mortality was definitely in the air. She had hit on the phrase The Great Australian Blight, G.A.B. for short, and she used it rather frequently in the course of the meal.

Later, with an agreeable sense of wallet and purse hardly at all depleted, they dawdled back to the Saracen's Head. They paused outside the Alhambra, a tiny theater, Victorian Moorish in design, a thing of many domes and minarets, which had been rescued from the degradation of Bingo when the festival first got under way. Here they inspected the poster for that year's operatic offering at the Ketterick Festival.

"*Adelaide di Birckenhead,*" read Gillian, shaking her head. "Never heard of it. Not that that says anything. Since they did *Anna Bolena* five years ago I haven't heard of any of them. They deliberately go in for the unknown, as we do on the drama side. The critics feel they have to come if it's the first performance for umpteen hundred years."

"*Adelaide di Birckenhead* has just got to be early Romantic."

"I should think so. It almost always is. You're right. '*Opera semiseria di Gaetano Donizetti.*' I presume that means we only have to take it semiseriously, which is a blessing. Who's in it? Oh—a Russian-sounding lady. She's never been here before. The tenor and baritone are old festival standbys, but they don't usually stay at the Saracen. The American tenor's rather dishy, but the Mexican's a nasty piece of work. God—I'm dying for a drink. Let's get back and see if I can find anyone I know."

The fact that the Shakespeare Bar at the Saracen was the one used by the festival people had nothing to do with any desire to pay tipsy tribute to the Swan of Avon. All the actors and singers who stayed at the inn had rooms on that side, the side where the balconies had been bricked in. The rooms on the other three sides had to be vacated for the duration of the festival, on the orders of the fire chief, so that members of the audience seated on the balconies could have unimpeded exit in the event of fire (in which case they would undoubtedly have been lost and frizzled in the maze of corridors). The Shakespeare was a big, warm, scarlet-velvet bar, with sofas and easy chairs, and its only disadvantage, that particular year, was its closeness to Reception. Des Capper alternated between the desk and the Shakespeare, where he hovered from table to table like an unappetizing headwaiter, determined to give more of his personal attention than anyone actually wanted.

At the bar a gaunt, harassed woman with pulled-back hair was worked off her feet. As she waited to be served, Gillian was delighted to see that there was someone she knew there. Ronnie Wimsett had been in two earlier Ketterick productions with Gillian, and his Theodorus Witgood in *A Trick to Catch the Old One* the previous year had been much admired. He was a rather plain young man by actors' standards, though wholesome and presentable in a middle-class sort of way. One's first instinct on meeting him was to put him down as a bank clerk or a clothes store assistant. It was only after talking to him for some time that one realized that this was the chameleon's self-protection. He had a talent for imitation and deadpan comedy that lit up his face and voice and a rubbery looseness of body that made him wonderful in farce. He was well into rehearsals, for he played the chaste apprentice himself.

"I shall say *nothing* of Jason's direction, nothing of his interpretation or of his understanding of my part in the play," he announced solemnly when Gillian and Peter had settled themselves down at his table. "Not because it's dreadful, you understand. But because you should come to your first rehearsal tomorrow with no trace of bias or *parti pris.*" He took a great draft of Saracen ale. "Let us instead while away the hours by ripping to shreds our fellow actors in the little-known masterwork."

Gillian smiled evilly, leaned forward, and the two went at it. Peter Fortnum, sitting on the edge of this gory arena, was interested and amused for a time, but his short career in the theater had left him with only a small circle of acting acquaintances, and after a time the names, their couplings and uncouplings, their tantrums and their delinquencies, began to pall. He was just beginning to wonder whether an obsessive interest in the marital affairs of the Galloways was not playing their game as they wanted it played, when he heard muttered words of Russian from the table beside him. He pricked up his ears at once.

Peter Fortnum was grateful to his minor public school for two things, and for only those two: These were the opportunities he had been given in the annual school play and the chance to learn Russian. Quite apart from anything else, the latter had given him quite spurious claims on any small parts going whenever anyone decided to do a Chekhov or a Gorki. He swung his chair around, chipping in a few words, and in no time at all he was sitting beside the star of *Adelaide di Birckenhead* and interpreting for her as she made her first real effort to communicate with the agent who had brought her to the West.

Natalya Radilova was slim, dark haired, and beautiful. She was also very much at sea. It was only her second time in the West, and her attempts to discuss financial and other arrangements with her agent had been hindered by the fact that she knew no more than twenty or thirty words of English. She had in all their preliminary communications pretended to a "competent" knowledge of the language, but her letters to him had in fact been written by a friend.

"I've arranged all this with your Ministry of Culture," her agent said somewhat wearily.

"Arrange it with me again," said Natalya.

The agent, Bradford Mallory ("Call me Brad") was, like the Galloways, something of a theatrical throwback, though in his case, Peter suspected, it was much more of a conscious act, for it had the label "performance" stamped on it, as theirs had not. He wore a cloak, he said "dear boy," and he occasionally patted the hand of the other singer on his books whom he had brought to Ketterick. This was the young man whom Mallory had apparently rechristened—"rather witty, wouldn't you say, dear boy?"— with the single name of Singh. An incredibly good looking young man, his Indian complexion had lightened from long, perhaps lifelong, residence in Britain. He said little, occasionally pouted, and sometimes smiled abstractedly at Mallory's affectionate advances. But what he did most often was to look at his reflection in the mirror on the wall behind Brad Mallory. When he had a clear, uninterrupted view of himself, he would put his chin up to pose in his most attractive position, pat his immaculately cut hair, adjust his tie, and then smile a catlike smile when the image presented to him was at its most pleasing. He was, Brad Mallory said, the coming countertenor, and he was to sing in the concert on the opening night of the festival.

As Peter Fortnum translated between Natalya and her agent—yes, she did know the role, yes, she did realize that, small though the theater was, the festival held a unique position in British musical life and success here could be a springboard for a very promising operatic career—he was conscious of a discordant presence in the vicinity, an intrusive note. The Australian voice has a cutting edge, admirable in the opera house but less well adapted to the social hobnobbing of a saloon bar. Des Capper was giving someone the benefit of his curious store of knowledge and opinions, which meant, in effect, he was giving them to everyone.

"Do you know that in Queensland they've got this new law forbidding hoteliers from serving sexual perverts?" There was a dirty little snicker. "Be a bit of a problem here in festival time, wouldn't it? Couldn't afford to lose half my customers." Peter half-turned his head and saw that it was the Galloways and Jason Thark whom Des was regaling with his muckiness. Peter's glance caught him gesturing in the direction of Brad Mallory and Singh, and he immediately changed his tone. "Mind you, I'm tolerant. Live and let live, that's my motto. I don't know if you've read about it, but it's been proved by scientists that sexual deviancy's purely a matter of brain damage during childbirth. Just like spastics. I know all about what causes spastics. Well, it's just the same with poofs, only more minor. It's like this…"

"Dear God!" breathed Mallory, raising his eyebrows to heaven with theatrical eloquence. "What have we done to deserve this antipodean clodhopper clumping all over our private lives and our personal sensibilities?"

He put his hand warmly on Singh's, but Singh's smile did not suggest that he had heard or, if he had, that he had understood. He said in an English that was perfect yet oddly inflected, addressing Mallory alone:

"Can we go up and watch the video? I've got *Little*

Lord Fauntleroy. You said we could watch it later tonight."

"And so we shall, dear boy, after one more little drinkie. It's my first chance to have a real talk to lovely, lovely Natalya, and she's full of questions that only I can answer."

Singh pouted but let himself be bought another sweet sherry.

Over at the Galloways' table, the theater's most glamorous couple had been stimulated by the company—though Des Capper was not in himself stimulating—to stage a public version of their afternoon row. It was a cleaned-up version, much more elegant, suggesting that they carried the idea of rehearsals and trial runs into other areas of their lives.

"We've never had any secrets from each other, nor from anybody else," Clarissa was proclaiming. "We take our pleasures when and where the fancy takes us. Of course it is a tiny bit unfair on Carston that all the people of real *weight* in the theater are men. Hardly any female producers, and the only kind of heterosex most of them are interested in is rape, and they're against it. And though Carston is not *averse* to men, as a variation, even he would hardly find the average impresario or producer attractive. Which leaves the balance of advantage very definitely on my side."

"And puts *me* very much in my place," said Jason Thark with a wide, untrustworthy smile. He was, in fact, a not unattractive man—broad shouldered, commanding. But he was—and he let you know it—a man to keep on the right side of.

"Darling, I'm honest with you, as with everyone else. You're really rather attractive, and I'd have slept with you even if you hadn't been our producer. On the other hand, that does add a sort of spice..."

Des Capper, watching them, had assumed an exquisitely misjudged air of being a man of the world.

"I've known plenty of couples in my time who had what they call nowadays an open marriage," he put in, bending forward confidentially. "It's nothing new, oh, my word, no! I was in India just after the war, and what I could tell you about the Mountbattens' goings-on would make your hair curl!"

Clarissa regarded him with the sort of look she might use to wither a bit player who had interrupted her big speech five lines too early.

"Which is why Carston, poor darling," she swooped on, "does *very* much prefer that we get work as a *couple.*"

"Though that's not so easy these days," Carston confided genially. "Playwrights aren't writing bitch parts for women as they used to."

"And why he himself has to make do for his sexual adventures with"—Clarissa's smile widened triumphantly as they were joined at their table by an inconspicuous young woman—"*awfully* promising young stage managers like Susan here. Susan, dear, we were just saying what a *won*derful job you're doing."

In the face of a smile which resembled that on the face of the tiger that had just swallowed the young lady of Riga, Susan Fanshaw sat down and said nothing. She was getting good at doing that with the Galloways. She had bought her own drink—for Carston Galloway was not a generous lover—and she had noted Clarissa eyeing her as she stood at the bar. Knowing Clarissa, she had realized she would be a target as soon as she joined them. She sat down with a mixture of unease and defiance. Jason Thark was more used to the Galloways and their social style, and he sat there, slumped, gazing about him with an easy tolerance. Des Capper, on the other hand, was beginning to feel ignored and made motions of moving on.

"Well, it's been nice having a chinwag," he said with a little wave of his pudgy hand. "Better get along to have a chat with some of the others in my little flock."

"Darlings, I had no idea he was a *cler*gyman!" floated Clarissa's voice after him, exquisitely modulated so that he could not avoid just hearing. "I would have tried to be polite to him if I'd known."

Des Capper, lips tightening, settled himself down at the next table. Nobody made any move to admit him, but somehow he managed to get himself in all the same.

"All settled in nice and cozy?" he inquired to a quartet of frozen faces. "Are the Russian lady and the Indian gentleman finding everything to their liking? They've only to give a shout if not and I'll personally see that something is done."

"Singh is English." Bradford Mallory sighed. "As English as I am—and rather more so than you. Natalya has not, so far, been able to express any discontents she may have accumulated, but she has now acquired an interpreter, so if she feels you don't warm the samovar sufficiently before you pop in the tea bag, she will be able—thanks to our *char*ming young friend here—to expostulate with you on the subject."

Des Capper blinked, as if he had been hit with a dictionary. But he was unputdownable, at the same time giving the impression that he was registering all the snubs.

"Ah—Mother Russia." he said with a sigh.

"Motherfu—? Oh, Mother *Russia.*"

"Mother Russia. It's an expression...sort of a nickname. It's a country that has always held a fatal fascination for me. The Winter Palace, Anastasia, *Battleship Potemkin...*

"'Lara's Theme,' *Gorky Park,*" murmured Brad Mallory.

"Exactly. It's a country of great elemental passions. I think I'd have been able to come to terms with it. The tragedy is, I've never been. I'd like to have told them a thing or two about how to run their agriculture. Ask the little lady"—he turned to Peter Fortnum, but he patted Natalya Radilova on the knee—"if they've ever been lucky enough to hear our great Joan Sutherland at the Bolshoi."

"Tell this stupid peasant to take his fat hand off my knee," said Natalya Radilova in Russian.

"Ah—she understood me. What did she say?"

"She asked you to take your hand off her leg," said Peter diplomatically.

Des Capper burst out into a chilling mine-host laugh.

"Well, well, well. No offense meant and none taken, I hope. I know they're a little puritanical still in these Iron Curtain countries. Me, I believe in being broad-minded. There's more than one kind of partnership, eh, sir?" Des gave a broad and repulsive wink at Brad. "If you ask me, the Russkies could take a few tips from your country, young man," he added, turning to Singh, who was lost in rapturous contemplation of the mirror image of himself sipping sweet sherry.

"Singh is English," breathed Mallory.

"The Indians know a thing or two about sexual tricks, eh? Not that we were in a position to cast the first stone as far as moral habits were concerned. We, the Raj, the ruling class, I mean. As I was saying at the next table, I was there in '46—7, aide-de-camp to the Viceroy—"

"*Aide-de-camp*, now?"

"That's right. And some of the goings-on and permutations and possibilities that I saw while I was with the Mountbattens you wouldn't believe. Still, when you went out among the natives—as I did, because I've got what you might call an inquiring mind, as you may have noticed—you saw things you'd never even *read* about. Even an old soldier like me had his eyes opened, I can tell you. Ever since then India has always exercised—"

"A fatal fascination?"

"It has. It's been calling me back—"

"Please. That chair. Madam—you are my soprano?" The voice—clipped, exact, icy—seemed to come from a great height. The young man was no more than six feet, but he seemed as high as the Matterhorn, and as daunting. He took Natalya Radilova's hand and, bending over, implanted on it a kiss, much as if he were stamping her passport.

"Gunter Gottlieb," murmured Brad Mallory with a pretense of enthusiasm.

It was a name more often breathed with devotion, even fanaticism, but that was always by people who did not know him, or need to. Orchestral musicians usually crossed themselves as they uttered the name or spat. Gunter Gottlieb had only recently become a name to conjure with in British musical life. He had been appointed conductor of the Midland Symphony Orchestra at the early age of twenty-seven. It was not, then, an orchestra with a great name. Mahler said that tradition is slovenliness; with the Midland Symphony Orchestra slovenliness was a tradition. Not any more. In a matter of months that mediocre band had been transformed by a mixture of sackings, threats, taunts, hectoring, and rehearsals that became torture sessions lasting well beyond the limits of endurance.

Now Gunter Gottlieb's concerts had become the talk of the Midlands and beyond. London critics traveled to Coventry and said that the young Austrian's Mahler was definitive for his generation. Old men wept at his Brahms and Schumann. Young girls waited outside the studios and concert halls for his autograph, undeterred by the open contempt with which he treated them. One or two of them would be selected for brief and violent couplings with the great man by one or other of the two thugs who, in imitation of more established conductors, comprised his embryonic entourage. Already the first records were in the pipeline. He was the talk of the musical world. It was a pity, everybody said, that he was such an unadulterated swine, but his music—!

Gunter Gottlieb had been in Ketterick a week. Des Capper—even Des Capper—knew his man. Without a word he vacated his seat and evaporated. Gunter Gottlieb sat down, knowing the chair would be there. His attendant heavy fetched him a drink and stood behind the chair looking menacing, though no more menacing than his master. Gottlieb sat in his chair, his back straight as a Victorian spinster's, his body seemingly bent by two perfect right angles at the knees and the buttocks. He fixed Natalya Radilova with his glassy, inquisitorial stare.

"You know your part?"

"Yes," said Natalya after translation.

"Perfectly? Including my embellishments for the cabalettas?"

"*Yes,*" said Natalya.

"You are late," accused Gottlieb, tight-lipped and schoolmasterly.

"Natalya, as you know," put in Mallory with an expression of tired courtesy, "was called in to save some performances of *Norma* in Cologne."

"Performances at Köln are no concern of mine. The production of *Adelaide* is. I was not consulted about your late arrival. Next year, when we perform *La Straniera*, I shall be in charge of *ev*erything: schedules, sets, costumes, production—and singers. Especially singers." He smiled his sunset-over-the-gulag smile. "No production can be perfect unless one man has total control. I have made it clear to the committee that I must have that control."

"I have no doubt you will get it," Brad said with a sigh.

"Is that quite understood? Now let us turn to your *aria di sortita* in the first act…"

He bent forward an inch or two, apparently in a gesture of intimacy, and went into lengthy instructions on how to phrase, project, and act during the heroine's opening aria. Any idea that this was hardly the time or place did not seem to occur to him. Peter Fortnum's powers as interpreter were taxed to the limit. Natalya listened with every appearance of attention. She was used to the ways of totalitarianism.

At the bar the gaunt, exhausted woman with the pulled-back hair, who incidentally was Des Capper's wife, was up to her eyes in orders. Des, however, was not in the business of helping behind any bar. He stopped by the table where Gillian Soames and Ronnie Wimsett were still deep in the entrancing business of character assassination. Nowhere, except perhaps the House of

Commons, offers more scope for that sport than the theater, and they were set fair to continue until the call for last drinks.

"Everything all right here?" Des asked, clearly intending to muscle in. "Anything I can do for you?"

Gillian Soames raised her head, clearly about to say, "Yes—piss off." But Ronnie Wimsett, a peaceable young man, took her hand in his, gazed adoringly into her eyes in the manner of a second-rate tenor in Act I of *Bohème,* then turned to Des and sighed. "No—everything is just wonderful."

There was nothing Des could do but leave them to themselves. He threw some orders at his drudge of a wife, then pottered off to his little office behind Reception, convinced that that pair were resuming an affair of long standing. It was one of a series of assumptions, some true, some false, that Des Capper made about his artistic guests. These assumptions soon attained in his mind the status of facts, as the many harebrained theories he read about in magazines did. They were stored up and gloated over, for Des was convinced in his mind that knowledge was power. It never occurred to him that knowledge was also danger.

Chapter 3

OPEN STAGE

The nature of Jason Thark's directorial gloss on that year's Ketterick Arts Festival play became clear to Gillian the next day. On the way down to breakfast on that, her first morning of rehearsals, she stopped to study a large poster in Reception detailing all the major events and the backup arrangements. Among these latter was a lunchtime lecture on *The Chaste Apprentice,* to be given by the lecturer in Gay Studies at the local polytechnic.

Whether the chaste apprentice of the play was gay in the modern sense of the word was open to question. That he was dreary in any sense of the word was incontrovertible. Gillian mentally reserved her position on whether the gloss could be made to work.

Behind the grand apron stage, now finally assembled, lay the magnificent and sprawling kitchens of the Saracen's Head as well as a couple of private dining rooms. When the festival began, the actors would take over the dining rooms as well as a good half of the kitchens. Until then the actors tended to lounge around in the yard as the play was being rehearsed or camp in the dining rooms where they could talk and laugh and quarrel with more freedom. Today was the first full stage rehearsal, and Gillian experienced the familiar lift of the heart when Clarissa Galloway, as Lady Melinda Purefoy, came on with Peter Fortnum as Peter Patterwit to begin the play:

> MELINDA: A private word, Sir, nothing else.
> PETER PATTERWIT: You shall fructify in that which you came for: your pleasure shall be satisfied to your full contention: I will (fairest tree of generation) watch when our young friend is erected (that is to say up)...

The authorship of *The Chaste Apprentice of Bowe* was a matter of some lethargic scholarly dispute. It was variously attributed to Dekker and Chapman, to Beaumont and Marston, to Beaumont and Massinger, and to Heywood and Middleton. It was generally agreed that two hands were discernible in it, though only half a brain.

At the lower level of the play the story line concerns the attempts of two apprentices, Peter Patterwit and Matthew Cotter (who is really Sir James Cotterel in disguise), to persuade the third apprentice, Simon Clear, to lose his virginity. At the same time, Sir James is being sought by his true love, Lady Melinda Purefoy, whom a family feud is preventing him from marrying. On the other level, the apprentices' master, Ralph Greatheart, the goldsmith, is resisting his wife's attempts to marry off their daughter, Allison (Gillian's part, and a lousy one), to an elderly aristocratic roué, Sir Pecunius Slackwater. At the end of the play the chaste apprentice loses his virginity to a whore in Deptford, Matthew is unmasked as Sir James (much to the chagrin of Mistress Greatheart, who would have consigned her daughter to him had she known), and Alison is given in marriage to Peter Patterwit, who is thus much too well rewarded for all his dreadful jokes in the course of the play.

Jason Thark's notion of how to ginger up the play was evident from the moment Ronnie Wimsett took to the stage as the chaste apprentice. He had been instructed to deck out his performance with every gesture from the camp repertoire: the fluttering hands, the swooping voice, the wiggled bottom, the mincing walk. It was pure sixties camp, an exercise in behavioral archaeology: Thus are homosexuals *not* played on stage today, and thus do they *not* behave. But Ronnie was a superb comedian, and the performance in itself was a riot. Gillian could see Ronnie making a great effect with it, which he could never have done with the lines as they appeared on the printed page:

SIMON CLEAR: Why sure, Madam, I will do it straight

was no great shakes as a line, yet said with a spaniel wiggle, a lewd gesture unseen by his mistress, and with vocal leaps worthy of a Mozart soprano, it was a surefire laugh getter.

Gillian also saw, of course, that as an interpretation it was open to several objections: The apprentice was supposed to be a dull young man, so that every other line Ronnie spoke and half the things that were said about him by others were contradicted by his physical performance;

this young man might be innocent of the knowledge of women, but chaste he could not conceivably be. In Jason Thark's reinterpretation the crowning episode with the whore of Deptford became no more than a brief shift of allegiance. Not that it mattered much; this was no masterwork. But homosexuals were these days as sensitive about their image as other minority groups. They could take against the production, and—remembering the usual makeup of the festival's audience—Gillian could imagine them banding together to form a fair-sized picket.

The idea that there might be some element of exaggeration and stereotyping in this performance got through even to Des Capper. On the second day of stage rehearsals he oozed up behind Gillian and Ronnie, while up onstage Carston Galloway, as Ralph Greatheart, was having a tremendous row with his (stage) wife. Having so much experience with his real one, Carston was making a great thing of it, and Gillian and Ronnie were talking in their normal voices when Des came up behind them and thrust himself uninvited into their conversation.

"That's a real little gem of a performance you're giving there," Des nasaled out, clapping Ronnie on the shoulder. "Got all the mannerisms fit to kill. I was pissing myself laughing back there."

"Thank you," said Ronnie briefly, unwilling to be rude to a man in his own courtyard.

"I wonder—don't mind me saying this, do you?— whether you've quite got at the psychology of the bloke. I wonder whether you're really living inside him yet, understanding what makes him tick. Ever heard of Stanislavski?"

"Didn't he compose *The Rite of Spring*?" said Ronnie brusquely, and marched backstage. Des nodded sagely.

"I think I got through to him," he said with grotesque complacency. "You could see he got my point. Though I think it was a quite different Stanislavski wrote *The Rite of Spring.*"

As the days of rehearsal flew by and the play took shape, both Gillian and Peter saw enough of the Galloways to wonder whether the balance of power—was that the word? of strength? of influence?—was quite as it had seemed to them on the day of their arrival. Gillian had seen the situation then as pretty much the same as when she had acted with them in a Haymarket revival of *The Rivals,* or two years previously here in Ketterick in *The Faire Seducer*; Peter, new to them, had seen it as the classic henpecked husband situation, though with a strong element of fighting back. Now they began to revise their opinions.

The first thing they noted was that Carston Galloway was giving a superb performance as Ralph Greatheart: warm, crusty, independent, salty. This was light-years away from the elegant, youngish man, cigarette holder in one hand, White Lady in the other, which was how the theatergoing public had hitherto seen him. Galloway was making the transition to being a good character actor. And like most actors, he knew his worth. Peter heard him one day when he took Jason Thark aside.

"Oh, Jason, that understudy to little Soames—is that still going begging?"

"Yes, we haven't got anybody."

"Then give it to Susan, will you? Susan Fanshaw. She's not really stretched by all these fiddling stage-management jobs."

Jason paused only for a second. "All right, Carston— gladly. Will you tell her?"

"If you like," said Carston, winking.

Whether Clarissa would ever make the transition to successful character actress could only be a matter for guesswork. What was sure was that she was not willing to make it yet. That really was the trouble: Melinda Purefoy was young love, she was romantic interest, she was dewy-fresh virgin. The actor playing Sir James Cotterel, with whom she was in love, was a public-school smoothie of twenty-six. Whereas Clarissa was— what? The reference books differed, or rather most of them kept silent, having no wish to give currency to Clarissa's blatant untruths. But the record of her career was public knowledge: She had made her West End debut in an H. M. Tennent revival of *Present Laughter* in 1962. Put her beside her supposed lover in the cruel light of day—which, after all, was what they would be acting under, with some blessed softening of evening light—and the gulf between them was brutally apparent. Put her, on the other hand, beside Constance Geary, a gin-ridden old bag whom everybody loved, who was giving a great performance as Old Lady Sneer, and you saw at once what Clarissa would become. Both were mature ladies at different stages of maturity. They were sisters under the gin.

Why she wanted to play the part was obvious—to prove she could still convincingly manage young women. It was as unwise an ambition as could be conceived, and how she had got the part was far from obvious. Gillian and Peter never saw any great evidence that her bedding with Jason Thark brought her tangible rewards in the way of added prominence or any shielding from his wrath. Could it be, then, that she had got the part because they wanted Carston for Ralph? Quite the reverse, in fact, of how she wanted people to see the situation.

Clarissa, however, was not to be underestimated, and she retained her unrivaled power of fuss making, which was legendary in theaters the length and breadth of the country. On Gillian's fifth day of rehearsals, during the midmorning break when everybody was in the little private dining room drinking coffee or something stronger, Clarissa burst in on them in a manner that certainly did not suggest she was going to ask whether anyone was for tenths. She used, in fact, her standard stage manner for delivering disastrous news or staggering developments.

"Really! It's too bad! Jason, you'll have to do something."

Jason was going over business with Ronnie Wimsett. He merely turned and raised a coolly inquiring eyebrow.

"It's that appalling Capper person. I've just been up to my bedroom—"

"Which one, darling?" inquired Carston languidly. "Ours or Jason's?"

"Ours, pig. And I found this...antipodean monstrosity poking around in my drawers."

"Underwear fetishist, would you say?"

Clarissa drew her hand across her brow. "God! Don't trot out all those ancient jokes, Carston. In the drawers of my dressing table. Actually poking and prying in them."

"Did you catch him in the act?" inquired Jason.

"Well, not quite," admitted Clarissa with a sigh designed to be heard in the dress circle. "One of those damned floorboards creaked just as I was opening the door. He'd got the drawer shut by the time I'd got into the room."

"What did he say?" Carston asked.

"He said he was just checking up on the maid's work." She put on a hideously nasal stage Australian accent. "'She's new to the job, y'see, and I'd like to be sure she's up to the high standards we set ourselves at the Saracen.'"

Jason shrugged. "Seems a fairly foolproof explanation."

"Oh, does it? Well, let me tell you, the maid who does our room every day, including this morning, was here two years ago when we were in The Faire Seducer. I count her as an old friend. She's just thrilled by anything to do with the theater. I gave her a pair of my stockings when we finished here last time—they do so appreciate something personal, these people."

This artless revelation of Clarissa's rather blunted the impact of her indignation. The assembled company was so staggered that the Galloways apparently tipped the hotel staff with items of their castoff clothing that they were unable for a moment to focus their minds on Des Capper's iniquities.

Constance Geary sighed and said privately to Peter Fortnum: "I wonder if I could tip my maid with my castoff gin bottles." Then suddenly a thought struck her, and she spoke up. "Oh—I've just remembered."

"What?" asked several people.

"Yesterday morning, when I was in the bathroom—making the best, darlings, of what never was very much—the maid came in and started doing the room. I sang away like mad, to tell her not to interrupt my mysteries. When I finally emerged, blushing all too artificially, she wasn't to be seen, and the door was open. So I poked my shy, virginal little head out, and there she was with this anthropoid Australian at the far end of the corridor. She had my wastepaper basket in her hand, and as far as I could see, darlings, they were actually *counting* the half bottles of gin in it."

"Really!" said everybody, laughing as they were intended to do.

"Perhaps they were thinking of sending your score to the *Guinness Book of Records*, darling," said Ronnie.

"But isn't it such *fun*?" exclaimed Connie. "What do you think he does with his knowledge?"

"Enjoys it?" suggested Jason.

"Oh, I rather hoped he might feed it into a computer or something so I could become a statistic."

Clarissa was annoyed at losing the limelight and annoyed that Connie had defused any anger she might have generated against their prying Mine Host.

"You call this *fun*?" she demanded with a vocal swoop reminiscent of an eagle picking up a lamb. "Fun? To have this *grubby* little creature scrabbling around in our private lives?"

"Well, it's hardly something we need to take seriously, is it?" Connie said reasonably enough. "It's a bit late in the day for me to go all coy about the fact that I spend much of my time pickled in gin. And you Galloways run much the most public private lives in the business."

"Carston and I have always been quite open about—"

"Yes, darling—spare us the party manifesto. Since you *have* been so open, what's the point in getting upset if this little Australian mole comes sniffing around in your underwear drawer? It's been washed in public often enough, heaven knows."

Clarissa shot her such a look that they resembled

nothing so much as two old bags in early Coward. She held her fire only because she knew Connie was a redoubtable opponent.

"What's he doing it for, that's what I want to know?" she asked, looking around. "What does he want?"

"It's for the knowledge," Gillian said. "It's a sort of instinct, and as Jason said, he probably just enjoys it—hugs it to himself, makes good stories of it after we're gone. He is unutterably loathsome, but he can hardly expect to be able to *use* things which none of us is trying to hide."

But Clarissa was far from being placated. "I think something should be done. You, Jason—you're the obvious one to do it. You could go direct to the festival committee. It's your first year here—you don't remember how wonderful it was at the Saracen in previous years. If something's not done quickly, the festival will lose all its spirit, all its old character. That man's got to *go*."

Jason took that point, at least, seriously. "I think, actually, you may be right. But the time to do something is not *now*. All we would achieve would be bad blood, recrimination, frustration. Not good for the show, for any of the shows. What might work is a collective letter, after this festival is over, from all the artists staying or working at the Saracen—a letter sent both to the festival committee and to the hotel chain that appointed him. Though what on earth possessed them to appoint him in the first place I can't imagine."

"Might one suggest blackmail?" said Clarissa sweetly.

"That's a point." Jason was thoughtful. "If so, we've really got a problem on our hands...Come on, boys and girls. Back to the grindstone. All onstage. We've really got to lick the brothel scene into shape."

Gillian had had to revise her opinion of Jason Thark as director somewhat. There were large areas of the play where he did, in everyone's opinion, excellent things. He worked tirelessly with Carston Galloway on the part of Ralph Greatheart, and together they created a rounded, human, and funny character from the bare bones of the script. He coaxed from Constance Geary, whose technique had been formed in proscenium-arch theaters, a performance that exploited all the potential of the apron stage. All the swirling crowd scenes, including the Deptford brothel one, went with great brio. The chaste apprentice as archgay seemed to Gillian funny but misconceived, and with Clarissa he could do nothing—but Melinda Purefoy was never going to be much of a part in anybody's hands. But all in all she had no doubt he was going to put together a real performance and probably have a critical success.

Of Jason as director, then, her estimate had risen. Of Jason as a person she felt she could reserve judgment. On Jason's intelligence generally, her opinion took a nosedive one evening. (She was sitting with Peter, Constance, and him at a table for four and telling them how much better the food at the Saracen used to be.) Suddenly Jason came up with one of his "ideas."

"I say, wouldn't it be effective if Singh could introduce each act with a few Elizabethan part songs?"

"With *what*?"

"Elizabethan part songs. I'll suggest it to Brad."

"I didn't know Singh was a ventriloquist," said Gillian. "I suggest you say Elizabethan lute songs."

"That sort of thing," said Jason blithely. "Something suitably bawdy could go down well."

Unfortunately the idea came to nothing. Singh had

such songs in his repertoire and had performed them in
Balliol College Hall and to other select musical societies.
But on the first night of *The Chaste Apprentice* he would
be performing Handel arias in an operatic concert in
Town Hall.

"The opening concert of the festival," said Bradford
Mallory. "A bit of a popular mishmash, to get audiences,
but I've persuaded some of the London critics along to
hear Singh. I am not having the dear boy dashing from
one end of town to the other to fit you in. But he could
sing on the other nights."

But Jason was only interested in the first night. That,
after all, was the night the critics came. As with Brad, it
was success with them that really counted with Jason.

"Rather typical," said Gillian. "And what appalling
ignorance in somebody directing an Elizabethan play. I
think he is essentially brilliant but vulgar."

She might, if she had thought about it, have admitted that this was a pretty good combination of qualities
for the director of a minor Jacobean comedy. But Gillian
was not disposed to like directors, and her nerves were
just a little bit on edge as the first night of the festival
drew nearer. So were all their nerves. The matter of Des
didn't help to keep them calm. They were all watching
him, wondering. More to the point, they felt him watching them. Few of them had any inhibitions about their
sexual lives, though few would care to conduct them
under the sort of spotlight the Galloways directed on
themselves. But it can be that the most lavishly open people in fact have corners in their lives that they reserve
from public scrutiny, and the grubby, obsessive nature of
Des's interest made them feel threatened. It was a rare
person who did not have a few private, personal things to

be cherished in solitude, blushed about, cried over in the dark.

Who could be sure that Des, in his snufflings in the undergrowth, would not find some path that would show him the way to those personal walled gardens?

Chapter 4

THE ALHAMBRA THEATER

Five days before the festival was due to begin, in thin afternoon sunlight, Peter Fortnum made his way through the streets of Ketterick towards the Alhambra Theater. The afternoon session at the Saracen was mainly to be devoted to scenes involving the Greatheart family, and he was not required until later. There were great stretches of the play in which Peter Patterwit did not appear, and contemplating the arid desert of smutty facetiae and labored puns that constituted the dialogue when he did, Peter was inclined to think the audiences might wish those stretches still longer.

On days when he was free he had got into the habit of going along to the Alhambra to see if he could be useful, which meant, in effect, to act as interpreter. Today, however, he had a more specific mission. He no longer looked at the silver-blue-and-maroon Moorish facade, merely nodded to the stage-door keeper, and forged his way unhesitatingly through the maze of cold, painted brick passageways to the backstage area. Today was to be the first full stage rehearsal with orchestra.

As Peter slid into the wings, he signaled to Natalya.

"Ah—Peter," she said in a pause.

"Oh, Peter—great," shouted Terry Potts, the producer. "Sit there at the side in case we need you, will you?"

Glad to be recognized and useful, Peter sat quietly in the wings and peered out into the auditorium. He recognized the director of the festival casting a benevolent eye over the second cornerstone of his two weeks of events. He saw Brad Mallory, with Singh, sitting in the third row and looking out for the interests of his other client performing at Ketterick. Very much his secondary interest, thought Peter rather bitterly.

He turned his glance back to the stage area and took in his first view of the set. The festival organizers had gone back to a designing pair who had served them well two years before for Donizetti's *Il Diluvio Universale* ("This is less a revival than a resurrection, in the Burke and Hare sense of the word"—*The Observer*.) Now they had constructed a permanent set with fragmentary bits of castle dotted around. It was handsome and serviceable, and splashes of color were provided by tartan wall hangings, for just as Bellini had called his opera set in Portsmouth *I Puritani di Scozia*, so Donizetti had apparently been convinced (or preferred to believe for romantic/commercial reasons) that Birckenhead was north of the border. Indeed, to him or his librettist all England seemed to be an appendage of Scotland, which at least righted a balance, some might think.

"With passion," shouted Gunter Gottlieb, a domineering intensity oozing from every pore. "This man is your lover and your king! Thrill your audience!"

For upstage had entered the handsome figure of the

Swedish-American tenor who was to sing Roberto il Bruce ("Broo-chay," as the language coach constantly insisted they all must call him). On stage Adelaide di Birckenhead, her husband Adalberto, and a motley collection of retainers and clansmen were about to launch into an exciting ensemble with choral backing. It was an ensemble that was later to serve for a vengeful heroine who had been abandoned in the catacombs in *Maria di Rudenz* and for conscience-tormented Christians and Romans in *Poliuto*, proving that Donizetti certainly recognized a showstopping tune when he hit on one.

"Now—passion!" shouted Gunter Gottlieb. "Controlled, thrilling passion!"

Adelaide di Birckenhead had had a history even more checkered than most of Donizetti's immense output. Composed originally in 1825 for the soprano Ferron and the castrato Velluti, it had been put aside when the latter deserted the company for meatier pickings in London. Later, at the height of his powers in 1835, Donizetti had unusually found himself without a libretto. "For God's sake write me a libretto," he had gone around frenziedly wailing to all his poet friends, displaying all the withdrawal symptoms of today's druggies. To no avail. He had had to reset almost the entire text of *Adelaide*, recasting Velluti's part for tenor. Unluckily, he had promptly forgotten about it in the excitement of composing *Lucia di Lammermoor*. Part of the manuscript score had lain for years in the Sterling Library in London, while the rest had been discovered only the previous year serving as a doorstop in the Conservatory of Music in Naples. This was to be its first-ever performance.

The story concerned a crucial moment in Scottish

history, which it travestied. It was said by one Italian commentator to have *"origine walterscottiana,"* a suitably vague description which obviated the need to ransack the works of the great unread Walter. The noble and patriotic Adelaide is unfortunate enough to be married to the skulking Adalberto, who supports the English tyrant Edgardo, who is busy suppressing the noble Scots. Adelaide is in love with the true Scottish king Roberto il Bruce, who is in hiding from the ravaging English armies. When he comes to *il castello di Birckenhead* in disguise, seeking succor, he presents her with a crisis of conscience which she solves spectacularly in the last act by hacking off her husband's head, then stabbing herself at the climax of a thrilling cabaletta. The stalwart clansmen of Birckenhead, typically willing to change sides at the drop of a coin, acclaim Roberto as their king.

The American tenor Krister Kroll stood at the Romanesque doorway at the very back of the stage, decked in furs left over from *Attila* ("proving that even Verdi nodded"—*The Observer*) in 1978 and tartan bought in bulk from the local Pricewise chain of discount stores. He was the only one in costume, because he said it was the sort of costume you needed to get the feel of. He was in the mold of so many American tenors: stalwart, clean limbed, and rather small of voice. He had appeared, pleasantly, in Rossini's *Torvaldo e Dorliska* ("a stillborn curiosity"—*The Observer*) the year before. As he stood, dramatically, at the doorway, first Adelaide whispered her apprehensions at the sight of her lover, then her husband expressed his suspicions at the sight (in furs and tartan) of the handsome stranger. And then Krister Kroll launched himself into the great tune:

Io son pari ad uom cui scende
Già la scure sulla testa...

Even to Peter, sitting in the wings, it was an anticlimax: It was like being handed lemonade when you had expected champagne. He saw the festival director mask an expression of dismay; he seemed to be wondering what sound, if any, would penetrate to the gods.

Gunter Gottlieb, with an impatient gesture, stopped the orchestra. Silently, pregnantly, he pointed with his baton to the center front of the stage. Krister Kroll looked uncertainly from Gottlieb to Terry Potts, the producer, in the stalls. Terry was already jumping out of his seat in agitation.

"But, Gunter, you can't have him there. He's just arrived, and he's apprehensive and agitated, uncertain of his reception. He can't just barge his way right to the center of things."

Natalya seemed to agree with him. She was expostulating violently in Russian against the improbability of the thing, which Peter was just about, somewhat nervously, to translate when he saw that Brad Mallory, with Singh in tow, had come on to the stage and Brad was expostulating with her and calming her. He seemed to be able to do it without benefit of common language, but that was doubtless a necessary talent of agents.

None of which cut any ice at all with Gunter Gottlieb. He pointed icily once more to center stage. Nervously, Krister Kroll moved forward.

"Now again from the soprano."

The annoying thing was that the man was undoubtedly right. You couldn't have the opera's one big moment, comparable with the Sextet from *Lucia*, go by default because the tenor couldn't be heard. Now Kroll rang out sweet and true, lacking only that dash of kingly swagger and animal excitement that the part seemed to demand. In a conflict between what made musical sense and what made dramatic sense, the music had to win. And yet, and yet...

"Now," said Gottlieb, stopping the orchestra at the end of the number and gesturing to the producer as if he were a dog he was sending to retrieve a partridge, "now you rearrange the staging."

And with a sigh the poor man, knowing when he was beaten, did just that.

"All right, if we must, we must. Yes, I know it's improbable, Natalya. I agree with you, darling. But you'll have to go *there*, center left, and..."

"I know how he feels, poor bastard" came a voice behind Peter's shoulders. He turned and was astonished to see the figure of Des Capper arriving in the wings. His eyes gleamed brightly with malice as he contemplated the scene. "Been a bit of a brouhaha, has there? Looks like it."

Peter, for some reason that he could not analyze, did not want to swap derogatory opinions of a fellow artist with Des Capper. Gottlieb was a bastard, but a brilliant bastard. He merely said: "They're just having to rearrange the positions a bit."

"Looks like there's been a good old-fashioned blowup to *me*. I know the signs. That swine has got the light of battle in his eyes. I know just how that producer must feel."

"Oh, yes?"

"*Just* how he feels. I've felt his nasty tongue myself. He's got no thought for the feelings of others. I'm sensitive. I don't like being spoken to like I was dirt."

Peter did not comment on Des's sensitivity. "What are you doing here?" he asked.

"Oh, I'm committee. Ex-officio as landlord of the Saracen. I've a right to go anywhere—" He suddenly caught sight of Singh, still onstage with Brad Mallory. "My! I see they had Indians in Birckenhead even then. Running the corner shops, I suppose."

Peter turned away with a grimace of distaste and didn't bother to correct him. He wondered about Des's right to go anywhere. It wasn't a right that any other member of the committee seemed to exercise. Peter turned back to the stage. Gunter Gottlieb, on the podium, was softly tapping his baton on the score. His expression suggested that he was long-suffering but had been pushed near the limits of even his saintly endurance.

"Now," he said when Terry Potts paused for breath, "is all clear? We go from there to the end of scene."

It was only ten minutes of music, but it seemed endless to Peter. The ensemble developed into a big scene of suspicion and suppressed fears, with every character generously sharing his innermost feelings with the audience. The problems of balance were acute, not least because of Krister Kroll's sweet but small tenor, which was swamped by the larger voices around him. Again and again Gottlieb stopped the music, reorganized the singers, hushed the orchestra, subjected Krister Kroll to heavy, biting irony, lathed the other singers, and ridiculed members of his orchestra. Even Peter felt himself sweating with tension. It was at the height of the unpleasant session, when the frayed tempers of singers and players were beginning to conquer their fear of Gottlieb and find open expression, that Peter from the wings saw Gottlieb's "heavy" sitting in the front row of the stalls, a slow, relishing smile on his face. He might not like music, but he certainly did appreciate aggro.

At long, long last Gottlieb called a break, and the tension dissolved. Peter's immediate visual impression was one of sweat. The orchestral musicians, jostling their way out through the door at the back of the pit, were shining with it, and one of the younger men seemed close to tears. The chorus members were bathed in it and wiping their foreheads, and the principals were drenched and close to the breaking point. Backstage everything became a jumble as singers and players made for the Green Room in search of cold drinks or chocolate to revive their strength. Peter was conscious of the Mexican baritone standing by a wall, clenching and unclenching his fists and muttering furiously to himself in the manner of operatic baritones. He was conscious in a far corner of the room of Krister Kroll being collared by Des Capper. Des had been in the Green Room when they arrived, making himself at home and waiting for a victim. The chain-saw voice cut through to Peter:

"You know, physiologically speaking there's no such thing as a small or a large voice. It's all a question of the diaphragm and the way you use it. If you'll take a tip from me..."

The American seemed to be a supernaturally nice person, for he was showing only small nervous signs of wanting to get away. Then Natalya Radilova arrived from the stage, and Peter darted away and took her aside.

"The message came through for you," he said in Russian. "It was 'Best wishes for rehearsals and the first night.'"

Natalya smiled, a smile apparently out of all proportion to the banality of the message. She squeezed Peter's hand, and they found themselves a private corner of the Green Room.

Once the chaos there had sorted itself out into groups, Peter and Natalya found themselves joined by Krister Kroll, still wiping the sweat from his open, engaging face.

"Who is that *creep* who got hold of me?" he demanded. "That schmuck? That smart-ass? I have never *heard* such crap as that guy was spouting."

"It's the landlord of the Saracen," said Peter. "A loathsome Australian by the name of Capper."

"I've known plenty of Australian singers," said Kroll, "and they've mostly been great people. But this, this—"

"It's not the nationality, it's the type. As with Gottlieb. Keep away from Capper. He's poison."

"Boy, am I glad I rented an apartment. I nearly went to the Saracen this time, to treat myself. But to have that creep giving me advice about breathing all day would—"

But he stopped, because heads were turning in the direction of the door, and conversation was stilling so that people could hear what was going on there. Gunter Gottlieb, alone of the performers, did not require sustenance or refreshment. His heavy had procured a soft drink for himself and was standing massively behind Gottlieb, doubtless to prevent a stab in the back. But Gottlieb had captured a prize: the director of the festival, who had been sitting in on the rehearsal after checking receipts at the box office. He had been hauled to the Green Room by Gottlieb with an end in view.

"Next year," said Gottlieb in his unattractive clipped tones, "we do *Fidelio*. People are waiting for my *Fidelio*."

"It's an idea," said the director in a practiced neutral voice. He was a local man, but one with long experience in arts administration. "Though of course we have tended to stick with the Italians. But next year's already tied up. We're doing *La Straniera*."

"I change my mind," said Gottlieb, putting aside *La Straniera* with a contemptuous sweep of the hand. "We do *Fidelio*."

"My dear chap, it's not on. Even if the committee were to agree—which I wouldn't bank on—it's still not on. You don't seem to understand the operatic world. All the worthwhile singers are booked up years in advance. All the principals for *Straniera* have been engaged. They'd hardly be suitable for *Fidelio*."

"I have my cast here," said Gottlieb, drawing a sheet of paper out of his pocket. "With alternatives if my first choices are not available. It is clear, yes? If you can get neither of them, you come back to me. Understood?"

"No, I'm sorry, old chap, it is not understood. There's no question of our upsetting our existing arrangements—"

It was at this point that Des bustled up.

"I wonder if I could mediate. As a member of the festival committee I think we ought to try to come to some compro—"

Gunter Gottlieb turned on him with a savage fury and pointed to the door.

"Out! Out! Out!" he bellowed. "I do not take advice from taverners! Get out and do not come near this theater ever again, is understood? You come near one of my rehearsals ever again and I have you removed, thrown out on your fat bottom. Is understood?"

Des had retreated three steps. When the heavy advanced from behind Gottlieb's back, he spluttered back any riposte and turned to slink out.

"No offense," he was heard to mutter.

Gunter Gottlieb turned back to the festival director, iciness reasserting itself.

"Is all your committee fools? They must learn to know their place. Now, as to *Fidelio*, I have a designer in mind..."

"Oh, my God," said Peter, pushing back his chair. "This bear garden makes life with Jason Thark seem a haven of rest. I must be getting back to the Saracen."

"Peter," wailed Natalya in Russian, "you're forsaking me. I have that dreadful finale to get through."

"Sorry, love. Duty calls. I was only given till four. They'll probably all be crying out for some fresh and engaging humor from Peter Patterwit..."

But they weren't, and he spent most of the rest of the afternoon and early evening lounging around, not unhappy to have escaped from the Alhambra. Gunter Gottlieb's plans for the festival were inevitably the topic of conversation in the Shakespeare Bar that evening. Gillian and Peter went out and bought a Chinese takeaway, enduring with sweet smiles the murderous glances from Des as they marched through Reception with the little cardboard boxes. Des, understandably, was looking murderous all evening. When they had eaten their fill in Gillian's room, they went down to the Shakespeare and found Natalya, Ronnie Wimsett, and Krister Kroll at a table together. The last named kept looking round nervously for routes of escape should Des feel impelled to come over and offer further advice on what he should do with his diaphragm. Gillian and Peter joined them, and soon they were well at it.

"It would change the whole character of the festival," Ronnie Wimsett said when he was told of Gottlieb's demands. He was a serious-minded, private young man, but he had come to feel passionately about the festival, to appropriate it in some way as a part of himself, as Gillian had. "The two things go together—Jacobean drama and nineteenth-century Italian opera. People like the music critic of *The Observer* sneer because it's not ear-wrenching stuff, but in fact it's wonderfully direct and passionate, really theatrical. And it's what people expect of Ketterick, what gives it its character. Give Gottlieb his way and it'll become just like any other festival. We'll be doing *The Marriage of Figaro* and *Pallyarse and Smellyhands*. and they'll be *his* Figaro and his *Pallyarse*. When that happens, we'll be just like any other festival. The next thing will be, he'll start dictating what plays are done, to tie in with *his* opera of the year."

"Still, the guy, though scary, has a way with him," said Krister Kroll ruefully. "What're the odds that Ketterick will not be doing *La Straniera* next year?"

"Never having heard it," said Gillian, "I can't weep bitter tears about the *specific* loss."

"Oh, it's great Bellini, and practically unknown. Even Beefy and Scrawny haven't recorded it."

Beefy and Scrawny, it was explained, were the currently highest paid tenor and soprano in the world.

"It's the principle I'm concerned about," said Ronnie.

"It's the personal level that concerns me," said Kroll. "It won't be the death of the festival if I don't come back, and I certainly won't while that monster is in charge. I'm a peaceful guy, but some of the things he said to me…"

Natalya Radilova, who was beginning to follow bits of conversation in English, went off into a bitter tirade in Russian. Peter paraphrased for her.

"She's complaining about my not being there when

she did her big final scene this afternoon. He was vile to her apparently. It's a difficult scene—It's where she brings her husband's head in on a platter and goes mad over it."

"My God!" said Gillian. "I thought this was supposed to be '*opera semiseria*.' I'd really hate to see a serious one."

"No, that's just another example of the amiable Gunter's influence," explained Kroll. "There are two manuscript endings, and they'd chosen the first. In that, some functionary comes along and explains that for unspecified reasons Adelaide's marriage has been invalid all along. Adelaide goes off to be Roberto il Bruce's queen amid general rejoicing, with only the baritone throwing a fit. That Mexican is awfully good at throwing fits. Anyway, along comes Gottlieb at the first rehearsal and says: 'No, we do the second.' In that one Adelaide hacks her husband's head off and then stabs herself after some fearsome coloratura. That's what Natalya is having to do. The annoying thing is that, as usual, Gottlieb is right. It's a much more effective conclusion."

Natalya went on at length in Russian. Peter explained. "Natalya says it is ridiculously difficult to do because it's so way out—so gory and savage. The audience will reject it at the drop of a hat, because it just seems impossibly savage."

Once again a familiar voice came from behind Peter's shoulder. He was beginning to feel he had a minor devil following him around.

"You wouldn't say it was impossible if you'd seen some of the things I saw in 1947, at the time of independence. Some of those poor bloody Indians had been so hacked about that their own mothers wouldn't have known them."

"Was this when you were viceroy?" Gillian asked sweetly. But Des did not appear to be listening. He was gazing ahead dreamily.

"Oh, yes, I've seen some sights, don't you worry." His eyes were on a far table, where Gunter Gottlieb was pontificating to the Mexican baritone and Brad Mallory. "I learned all you need to know in India about how to even scores."

Chapter 5

THE ALCOVE

A mist hung over Ketterick and the London suburbs around it as the first day of the festival dawned. During breakfast, though, it began to lift, and by ten the town was bathed in gentle sunshine from a pale blue sky.

The visitors were arriving, that was for sure. By now Ketterick was securely established in the festival catalog, cunningly poised to take advantage of that moment, around May to June, when longen folk to goon on artistic pilgrimages. By car and coach, by late-arriving trains from Newcastle, Bath, and Manchester, even by bicycle they came, changing the character of the complacent suburb. Some of the visitors were regulars, with their diaries already filled in and their seats booked; some came on spec and sat around in parks and squares going through the festival brochure to see what they might take in. There was the *Play of Daniel* in the ruins of Walsey Abbey, three miles out of town; there was Bruno Brazen, the well-known American organist and showman in St. Margaret's Church; there was a wispy French soprano singing wispy French songs; there was Morris dancing in the Queen's Square and a superb black dance group from Leeds in the Civic Hall. Tonight there was *The Chaste Apprentice* at the Saracen's Head and a popular operatic concert. Both these events were booked solid, but for the disappointed there was a beer race in the Ketterick football stadium. There was—as there was on that other pilgrimage, to Canterbury—something for everybody.

At one time or another during the day most of the new arrivals strolled into the Saracen's Head to look at the wonderful courtyard and stage. One of the hazards of this was that Des Capper was liable to sidle up with a proprietary air and ply them with information, advice, and cures for constipation. One of the American visitors, a lecturer in Renaissance studies at Kent State University, called him "a true English innkeeper" and "a real Harry Bailly after Chaucer's own heart"; but most of the rest sensibly ducked off to one or other of the bars. These were kept very busy, and Mrs. Capper in the Shakespeare was rushed off her feet, though help from her husband got she none.

If they were lucky, these stray visitors saw scraps of last-minute rehearsal. In the true spirit of the Elizabethan troupe, the cast was quite unembarrassed about putting finishing touches to the performance before future members of the audience, who marveled at the contrast between their apparel of jeans and T-shirts and their talk of ruffles and codpieces. The brothel scene had caused particular difficulty, being such a whirl of activity, and the casual dropper-in might see Peter Patterwit open that unedifying scene with Doll, the whore, indulging in some typically sparkling Jacobean wit:

DOLL: You, goodman swineface.
PETER: What—will you murder me?

DOLL: You remember, slave, how you abused me
      t'other night in a tavern?
PETER: Not I, by this light.
DOLL: No, but by candlelight you did...

Oddly enough, such samples did not put off most of
the visitors. Somehow the setting and atmosphere (or the
"ambience," as several of them preferred to put it) were
so exactly right for the play that many of them dashed
straight off to the festival box office to see what tickets
were available for later performances.

If Des was a hazard for the occasional visitor, he
was an ever-present danger to the performers and residents. It was, after all, his first festival, and he naturally
wanted to see everything he could. Unfortunately, he
wanted to be part of everything, too, and there was
abundant evidence that despite his recent rebuff at the
Alhambra, the start of festivities had gone to his head.
He was liable to pop up everywhere, poking his nose in
and having his little word of worthless commendation or
erroneous advice to all and sundry. Few were polite
back, but he gave no sign to their faces of having registered their contempt.

Constance Geary's part as Old Lady Sneer was not a
large one. She played a cousin of Sir Pecunius Slackwater,
dragged into the marriage negotiations. Her performance
was already a matter of well-routined gestures and
intonations, and she left it to younger generations to over-
rehearse. She sat around in various parts of the Saracen's
Head, holding court and allowing visitors to buy her
drinks. Sometimes she could be found on her own in the
little alcoves and open spaces that the inn abounded in,
quite happy with her memories and her gin bottle. She

also noticed a lot more than might have been thought, though she would have been hard put to order it in any way in her mind. It was nearly lunchtime, in one of those alcoves, apparently deep in thought after a copious swig from her bottle, that she saw Des Capper coming.

"All on your own-e-o?" he asked with his horrible brand of jocularity.

"Trying to be," said Connie.

"They can get tiresome, can't they, actors?"

"*We* can. But then so can most people."

"What I mean is," said Des, leaning closer, Connie thought to catch the smell of her breath, "you can have too much of them. They tend to emote is how I'd put it. Those Galloways, for example. Always at it, aren't they?"

"At it? You mean like Alice?"

"At each other's throats might be a better way of putting it. Morning, noon, and night. And both of them having a bit on the side and talking about it openly. Jeez, I don't know; it's not my idea of a marriage."

"My dear man, I've known more different kinds of marriage than I've had hot dinners. There are as many recipes for a good one as there are for a bad one."

"What makes them stay together, that's what I wonder. Why stick it out?"

"I imagine it must be because they rather like it."

Des looked at her, then shook his head with wonderment. "Then there's young Peter Fortnum. He's up to something, that I do know."

Connie Geary paused, looking at him contemplatively. She took her bottle out of her handbag, had a swig, and replaced it. Then she looked at Des again. "I presume we are now changing the subject, am I right? Because Peter Fortnum hardly comes under the heading of actors who emote. Indeed, he is an exceedingly quiet young man, which is pleasant but unusual. A youthful Alec Guinness, no less. So we are now discussing what he is up to, and I must confess I have no idea. Do you mean to ask if he is sleeping with the charming but impenetrable Russian lady?"

"Oh, as to that, maybe, but I think not," said Des, rubbing his hands together. "But there's something going on, and I think it might be a sight more interesting than them sleeping together."

"I'm glad to hear it. At my age there are a lot of things more interesting than sex, though I'm not sure there ought to be at theirs. Have you any idea what it is?"

"Oh, I've ideas all right. There's no flies on me, you know. I'll get to the bottom of it."

"This is fascinating," said Connie. She sat there hoping she would remember enough of this conversation for it to form a vital piece in the complaint to the committee when the present festival was over. She even decided to stop sipping from her bottle, to keep her head clear. "Is there anyone else at the Saracen in whom you are taking a special interest?"

"Oh, lots," said Des, leering. "A student of the human condition, that's me." He leaned forward. "Know how that Kraut conductor gets his girls?"

"He's Austrian. Not that anyone imagines *that* makes much difference after the Waldheim business."

"Right. Same difference, that's what I say. Well, do you know how he gets his girls?"

"Animal magnetism?"

"His heavy recruits them for him. Just like that. He puts the proposition, then they're taken up to his room for a quick you-know, then they're out. He picks them out from among Krauty's fans. Doesn't pay them, either. I expect they form themselves into a sort of club or have a special tattoo or something."

"I did hear whispers about that," said Connie with a shiver of distaste. "It *is* rather disgusting."

"And I'll tell you this: He likes them young. The younger the better."

"'His favorite form of sinning is with one who's just beginning'," sang Connie, from the Catalogue Aria.

"That's it. That's just about it. If I could catch him with one who was below the age of consent…"

"Yes?"

"That would do the trick…Trouble is, at that age they're not usually interested in classical music, are they? And the heavy tells me he's very careful."

"You'll have to find something else, then."

"Yes, I will, won't I?"

"And is there anyone else of us that you have your eyes on?"

"Oh, yes. Oh, there definitely is. No question about that…" Connie sat there quiet, but a cunning expression came into Des's eyes. "But that would be telling, wouldn't it? You're not going to draw me out on that."

With a sigh, Connie took out her gin bottle. "You know what that stuff does to your kidneys, don't you?" asked Des. He went on to describe it in detail before leaving with a wave and his favorite addendum: "Don't mind me telling you, do you?"

Onstage they were rehearsing a quarrel between Sir Pecunius Slackwater, suitor to Alison Greatheart, and the whore of Deptford, who was an old acquaintance.

SIR PECUNIUS: Out, you babliaminy, you unfeathered, cremitoried quean, you cullisance of scabosity!

WHORE: Good words, Master Slackwater, to speak before a maid and a virgin.

SIR PECUNIUS: Hang thy virginity upon the pole of carnality...

By the wall of the courtyard, Natalya, in slacks and jumper, was standing in a patch of sunlight near the windows of the Shakespeare Bar. She was beginning to tap her feet and look anxiously at her watch, but then she saw Peter Fortnum coming through the great gates from the High Street.

"Did you get through? Have they arrived?" asked Natalya urgently in Russian.

"No, there's been some confusion about times. The party's not due for another hour at least."

"Oh, my God."

"I think it's a genuine confusion. There doesn't seem to be any doubt they will arrive."

"I've got to go. I'm due at rehearsal in ten minutes."

"I know. I'll stick around and ring them again in an hour or two."

"Will you come and tell me?"

"Yes, if I can. I don't *think* I'll be needed to rehearse here, but you never know what people may take it into their heads to want to go over. But I'll try."

"Please come if you can. *Please*, Peter."

"Of course. You know I will. And it'll be all right."

He took her hand, but they sprang apart as they heard an involuntary cough close to Natalya's ear. Des Capper was standing just inside the open window of the

Shakespeare Bar. From the expression of extreme frustration on his face it was clear that the fatal fascination that Mother Russia had always had for him had never induced him to learn her language.

In the street near the Alhambra Theater the big man with the Midlands accent was approached by a girl.

"Excuse me, but you're Gunter Gottlieb's bodyguard, aren't you?"

He looked at her appraisingly. "Something like that."

"It's just that…he's always in such a hurry after rehearsals…and I wondered if you could…get his autograph for me."

She proffered a book. It looked very new. The big man did not take it.

"Maybe I could…And maybe I could go even better."

"Really?"

"Maybe I could arrange a…meeting."

She smiled up at him, looking all of fifteen. "I wondered if you could."

"At a price, of course."

The operatic offerings of the Ketterick Festival were never premiered until the second or third night. Nothing was allowed to draw attention from that year's play. Maybe in future years Gunter Gottlieb would change all that, but he had not done so yet. By tradition the musical event on the first night was something undemanding: a Viennese night, a Gilbert and Sullivan evening, a nice bit of Tchaikovsky. This year it was a popular operatic concert. Gunter Gottlieb, needless to say, would have nothing to do with it.

Thus, the final rehearsal with the Midlands Orchestra in the Town Hall was under the command of a pleasant young man who had done well in a recent conductors' competition. They'd put together a very nice program, with an overture by Rossini, some ballet music by Verdi, and lots of standard arias. Natalya was singing *"Vissi d'Arte"* and the letter scene from *Eugene Onegin*, the Mexican baritone was spitting out Iago's *"Credo,"* and Krister Kroll was singing an aria from *Faust* that the program, through slovenly proofreading, referred to as *"Slut! Demure, chaste et pure."* Singh's arias had presented more of a problem, since the countertenor repertoire hardly counted as popular opera, but Brad had hit on two surefire Handel arias, and these he was to sing in the first half. Brad had insisted he was to *conclude* the first part of the concert, knowing that the scope for excitement and applause would be the greater if there was nothing coming immediately after.

Natalya was finishing the letter aria in a glorious flood of sound when Peter arrived at the Town Hall. He listened approvingly. He was no expert on music, but he knew a good sound when he heard one. It was a very informal rehearsal, and the Town Hall was dotted with people. Peter was pleased to note approving glances going from person to person. Natalya came off the platform and into the body of the hall, looking around for him. He put up his hand, and she came over to him.

"I got through," said Peter.

"And?"

"They'd just arrived."

Natalya did not allow herself any obvious expression of relief, but Peter could see her tension relax.

"All of them?"

"Yes, all of them. I spoke to him."

"Oh—marvelous."

"He sent his love."

"Only three more days now."

Onstage Singh had launched into Caesar's aria with horn obbligato from *Giulio Cesare*: "*Va tacito e nascosto.*" His rich, agile voice was filling the Town Hall effortlessly and weaving brilliant patterns with the horn. Brad Mallory, sitting in the middle of the hall, looked to be purring.

"What an extraordinary voice," said Natalya.

"Quite amazing."

"What else did he say?"

Peter looked around, instinctively cautious.

"It's all right," said Natalya. "I'm sure that dreadful man doesn't speak Russian. I could see it in his face."

"No, I don't think so. Anyway, he's over there."

And as Peter launched into an account of what had been said on the phone, he looked toward the back row of seats where Des had ensconced himself, exercising in the absence of Gunter Gottlieb his right as a member of the committee to go anywhere and see anything. He was gazing ahead of him, almost dreamily, with a smile of pure, luxuriating pleasure playing on his lips.

Chapter 6

THE HIGH STREET

Performances of *The Chaste Apprentice of Bowe* began at seven o'clock. Everything at the Ketterick Festival began early, for many members of the audience were not staying in Ketterick but came from other suburbs and were nervous about traveling on bus or underground late at night. So at six the great gates of the Saracen's Head were closed, and the small door cut into the right-hand one was opened for the collection of tickets. Everyone, even those seated on the balconies, went through this gate, and the ticket collector stationed himself there from six onward. All the bars were closed to members of the general public until after the performance was over—enough to do to serve the players and the audience. Frank, the hotel's commissionaire, stood by the main entrance to the hotel, to the right of the gates, to stop anyone who might try to get into the play without paying by slipping through Reception and then through the Shakespeare Bar.

Once through the little door in the great gates, the audience, chattering and laughing and sure they were in for a rather special experience, separated up, some going to one or other of the bars, some to sit in their seats and read their programmes, some merely to sit and soak up the atmosphere of the great courtyard. Those who had seats on the balconies had directions on how to get to them on the backs of their tickets—directions which mostly added to their confusion, so indescribable were the complexities of the Saracen's Head.

Behind the stage, in one half of the enormous kitchen, and screened off from the rest, the actors changed. The women had the private dining room next to it, but coming and going between the two was frequent and unrestricted. Costume was important in the Ketterick plays, for splendor and variety of dress provided the feast for the eye that compensated for an otherwise bare stage. No producer—not even Jason Thark—had yet suggested a modern-dress production at Ketterick, and anyone who did would have been firmly rebuffed. The stage demanded ruffs and bodices, buskins and codpieces.

Fish was being served in the dining room that night. The smell penetrated into the dressing rooms and provoked feeble witticisms like "Odds fish!" A limited meal was provided for the few residents not involved in the play and the richer members of the audience. Late-night snacks would also be served after the performance: lasagna, fish pie, or risotto. Most people, though, contented themselves with drinks.

They were pleasantly busy in the Shakespeare Bar. This meant that Win Capper was run off her feet. Hair drawn back, unhealthily sallow, she somehow looked like a woman who had been run off her feet since girlhood.

"Des," she called, unusually daring, when she saw her husband going around the bar doing his Harry Bailly act among the early arrivals for the performance, "do you think you could come behind the bar and help out for a bit?"

Brad Mallory, sitting at the bar, thought this must be an unprecedented request. He had never seen Des giving a hand at anything around the hotel except Reception. Certainly Des received the request gracelessly, casting his eye up to heaven and taking his time in getting behind the bar.

"Des," said his wife, working on an order for three different beers, "you're going to have to come and help at Interval. I'm not going to be able to cope."

"You'll have Dawn from the kitchen to help you," said Des, pouring soda into a whiskey in an infuriatingly leisurely manner. "There are three other bars for people to go to, for Chrissake."

"The Shakespeare's the biggest and most popular. There's only twenty minutes, and people have to have time to drink their drinks. You'll have to come and help."

"All right, little lady," said Des, leering around at a sea of proffered flyers. "Your wish is my command."

"No, I *mean* it, Des. I need you here."

"And I'll be here. Am I in the habit of not meaning what I say?…I ask you, Mr. Mallory, don't I usually mean what I say? Now, what can I get you?"

Outside in the main entrance Frank, the commissionaire, was getting bored. There was a steady queue waiting to go through the little door into the courtyard, but nobody was attempting to sneak past him into the body of the hotel to get an illicit view from somewhere or other. This was not surprising, as he was six feet two and built like a barrel. The only residents in the hotel at the moment were the festival people, in the rooms over the Shakespeare. Any other would-be guest who had arrived in Ketterick without a bed was turned away by Frank with a word, courteous but final. In fact, there was nobody manning Reception, because there was no point in it. Des had assigned the girls there to other work for the duration of the festival. Frank thought it very dull, really. Still, soon, when the play started, he could walk along and have a chinwag with Bob, the ticket collector on the gate. They were good friends and usually talked the play away during festival time. Unless, this year, that Australian twerp should take it into his head to put a stop to it.

The poncy Mr. Mallory—Frank had got *his* number—had come mincing out of the Shakespeare and now came through Reception, looking pale but not interesting. He nodded to Frank as he came through the main entrance and headed off in the direction of the Town Hall, clutching his cloak around him. A *cloak* for God's sake...Des Capper came out almost immediately after.

"I've been helping in the bar," he announced to Frank, as if it were a newsworthy event. "Helping the little lady. Now they're all taking their seats. I think I'll slip in at the back and watch the first few minutes. Mind you, I think I've got *this* play's number, by seeing the rehearsals. It's no literary masterpiece, you take my word for it. Still, as a member of the committee, it's as well to see how the audience is taking it."

And he rambled through the little door into the courtyard. Frank gave a meaningful stare, of skepticism verging on contempt, at Bob, standing in the street by the door and taking tickets. So long a stare was it that he nearly missed seeing a young woman going through the main door of the hotel. He hotfooted it back to the door and into the open area around Reception, but by this time the young woman had crossed it and had gone, not to the Shakespeare Bar but to the stairs leading to the bedrooms.

"Can I help you, miss?" Frank called.

The girl turned round. She was a cool, fresh little thing, in a bright summer frock—and not much else, Frank guessed. Frank was an ex-soldier and experienced in such matters. A tingle stirred his old blood. She looked about fifteen, he thought, but when she spoke her voice was not a schoolgirl's.

"No. No, I don't think so."

It was an attempt—and not a bad one—at upperclass impertinence. Frank bristled.

"The play's about to start, miss, and the bars and dining rooms are shut, and—"

"But I'm not going to the bars or dining rooms, am I?"

"Would you mind telling me, miss, where you are going?"

She left a cool pause before she replied. "No, I don't mind. I'm going to see Gunter Gottlieb. You know, the great conductor."

"Ah." Frank did know. There had been other young ladies. "Mr. Gottlieb's not occupied with festival stuff, then?"

"No, evidently not, I should have thought. I have an appointment with him."

"I see. Very well, miss. Sorry to have troubled you."

She smiled at him, a practiced ingenue smile. Then

she turned and went up the stairs. Shaking his head gently, Frank went back to take up his position outside the main door. The evening was clear and sunny, and both Ketterick folk and visitors were strolling along the High Street, window-shopping, eating ice cream, flirting and hoping to be flirted with. The odd car drove past, but no heavy trucks. They were banned from the center of Ketterick during the hours from seven to ten at festival time. Only heavy trucks could have made any impression through the massive gates of the Saracen's courtyard. Cars, Frank knew, made no disturbance at all.

A fragment of the play wafted out to him. That meant the ticket gate had opened:

> RALPH GREATHEART: I hope to see thee one o' the monuments of our City, and reckoned among her worthies, when the famous fable of Whittington and his puss shall be forgotten, and thou and thy deeds played i' thy lifetime by the best companies of actors, and be called their get-penny…

So the first scene was over, and Carston Galloway was on, inciting the chaste apprentice to City greatness (with Ronnie Wimsett looking and acting about as unlike a City worthy as it was possible to get). Frank had timed things in dress rehearsal, and he knew this meant the play was ten or twelve minutes in. Turning his eyes, he saw that Des Capper had emerged through the little door in the gate and was now closing it.

"Ah, well, it's going very much as I expected," he said judiciously when he came up to Frank. "Quite nicely on the whole. Whether that mob knows what they're laughing at is another matter, but so long as they think they're enjoying themselves, that's the main thing. Make 'em laugh, make 'em cry, eh? I haven't read up much about this opera they're doing yet, but I expect it's the same principle there. That's show biz, the world over...Well, I'll maybe look in during the second half to see how it's going. Meanwhile, I'll be in Reception if I'm wanted, Frank."

"Right you are, sir."

"Or up in the flat. Call up the stairs if I'm wanted. Keep on the door the whole of the first half. We don't want any gate-crashers seeing the play for free."

"Right. Oh, by the way, there was a young girl, sir..."

"Oh?"

"But she was a guest of Mr. Gottlieb's..."

They looked at each other, and Des laughed lasciviously. "Someone should have told me that at festival time this place doubles as a brothel."

He winked and chuckled, as if that were a high honor. Then he went in and turned towards the reception desk, apparently in high good humor.

For a few minutes Frank stood just inside the door, looking out, hearing Des fiddling around on and under the desk. Then Des went into the manager's room behind. Frank nonchalantly went through the door into the street and stood for a few minutes there. The characters had changed a bit from a half hour earlier, but the activities were much the same. As a spectacle it lacked variety. So, giving a nod to his friend Bob, who was standing by his little door, they met halfway, towards the end of the hotel wall. From here they could both keep an eye on their respective doors, yet there were no open windows to inhibit them from launching into a fine old discussion. Men, contrary to general belief, are much the best gossips, and the festival and its artists always provided these two with ample manure to spread. Every year it was the same, and they went at it with a will.

The first interruption came when they were just five minutes into their chat and hardly beginning to disentangle the marital and extramarital affairs of the Galloways. The girl who had gone up to Gunter Gottlieb's room came prancing out again.

"*Good*-bye," she called, waving.

"Well, *she* didn't take long," said Bob.

"They never do," said Frank. "It's in and out."

"Perhaps he pays them by the minute."

"And perhaps he doesn't pay them at all. We'll come to Mr.—I beg his pardon, *Herr*—Gottljeb in a minute. But as I was saying…"

In the Town Hall concert the Mexican baritone was giving the audience his Iago. It was a part to which he was suited, if you regarded Iago as a snarling, spitting, teethbaring villain who could never have convinced anyone for two minutes that he was a good chap. But his enunciation of belief in eternal nothingness was getting through to Brad Mallory. At any rate, he was sweating. Sitting there in his aisle seat, he was sweating profusely. What was next? The march from *The Trojans*. Then little Natalya in the letter scene from *Onegin*. After that would be the time to slip out. Anyone who knew him would assume he had gone backstage to congratulate her. Or to spur on Singh, who was on soon after. There was that phone box just outside the Town Hall. Please God it would not be occupied.

Brad Mallory sat on and sweated. Never had the Trojan March seemed so long.

Frank and Bob had a long, uninterrupted chat during which few of the performers staying at the Saracen came off unscathed. It was only at a quarter past eight that Frank looked at his watch and shook his head.

"Blimey. Quarter past eight. Interval in fifteen minutes or so, I should guess. Better get back to my post."

He looked around him, like a diver coming up for air. Approaching along the High Street was Bradford Mallory, clutching his cloak about him, though the evening was still warm.

"Concert over, Mr. Mallory?" Frank asked, back at his post at the entrance. Brad Mallory fluttered.

"The first half. That was all I'm interested in. Singh sang divinely! He had a phenomenal success!"

"I'm glad about that, Mr. Mallory." The romantic figure, having poked his head into the Shakespeare and then come out again, disappeared up the stairs. Frank repeated sardonically under his breath: "I'm *very* glad about that!" Then he went outside again and made a gesture to Bob at the ticket door which said, as plainly as talking, "These artists!"

Behind the stage, in the screened-off part of the kitchen that was the men's dressing room, the members of the cast that were not onstage sat in dim light, listening to the performance.

"It's going well," said Gillian Soames.

"Very well," said Ronnie Wimsett. "They're laughing at the jokes."

"And at a lot of things that aren't jokes at all."

"That's natural," said Jason Thark pedantically. "We get further and further away from the Elizabethan language. I sat through a performance of *Macbeth* last year and realized I understood less than I did when I saw it as a teenager."

"That's because nowadays we play the Bard complete and gabble him," Connie Geary pointed out. "In the past they cut him and spoke him properly."

"At least no one seems to have taken offense at the chaste apprentice," said Ronnie. "That's a relief."

"That's because we made him so far out he was a parody of a parody of a homosexual," said Jason, still with his schoolmasterly manner, which was perhaps a sign of nerves. "That was my intention all along."

"The amazing thing is, they're even laughing at Peter Patterwit," said Connie Geary in her rich, throaty tones. "He's the sort of Elizabethan character who makes me groan and switch off the moment he sets foot onstage."

They were silent, listening to Peter Fortnum, who was doing his stuff onstage.

PETER PATTERWIT: Why, sure my blood gives me I am noble; sure I am of noble kind, for I find myself possessed with all their qualities: love dogs, dice and drabs, scorn wit in stuff-clothes, have beat my shoemaker, knocked my seamstress, cockolded my pothecary, and undone my tailor. Noble? Why not?

"He's doing a good job, that lad," said Carston Gallo-way. "He's got the projection for it, so he gets the mean-ing across, however feeble it is."

"Oh, God," said Connie Geary suddenly and loudly.

"Shhh," said Jason.

Connie was rummaging frantically in her bag, which she carried around with her everywhere.

"Darlings, I've never done that before. I've run out of gin. Somehow or other I've forgotten to put my second half bottle in my bag. I was sure—"

"Do you want me to get some more for you?" asked Peter Fortnum, who had just come offstage and was beaming with pleasure at the experience of an audience that was with him.

"I'm not on again before Interval."

"But *can* you?"

"Of course. I can go through the kitchen and dining room and into the Shakespeare Bar. Or shall I go up to your room and get you a half bottle?"

"Darling, could you? You angel. Because we have *hours* to go yet, and bar measures go very little distance. The halves are all set up on my dressing table like a line of soldiers. Here's my key. It's the first floor."

"I'll find it," said Peter.

But the Saracen has ways of defeating people who say that. At any rate, he seemed to be away an awful long time, and when he returned, Connie was wailing that she felt like the Sahara Desert at the height of the season. Peter was out of breath and explained that he had got utterly and completely lost. By then Carston Galloway was onstage, with Mistress Greatheart, Alison, and Sir Pecunius Slackwater in a tremendous quarrel scene that concluded the first half. The Interval was upon them, and the audience sounded good-humored and nicely thirsty as they hotfooted it to the bars.

In the Shakespeare Bar tension had been rising as the Interval approached.

"Well, the glasses are all ready," said Win Capper, looking at her watch. "Interval's supposed to be at half past. Fifteen minutes to go, if they stick to their times. *Which* they won't, knowing these artistic people. No consideration, as a general rule. Still, I think you could go and get the snacks from the kitchen. Here, take this tray."

Dawn, roped in as the best of the dining-room staff, trotted off to get the little plates of savory this-and-that's which were to be set out on bar and tables in celebration of *The Chaste Apprentice*'s first night. When she got back, she found that Win had poured out a large number of red and white wines and some gins and whiskeys.

"They're the staples," she said. "You can't go wrong pouring them in advance. And we'll be rushed even with Des here. If they want ice, they'll have to serve themselves with it. Now let's put the snacks out."

In the event, Interval started only three or four minutes late. "I expect Des is watching from the window," Win said, "and he'll dash through when it starts." But when the great mass of the audience from the courtyard began to stream into the Shakespeare, saying things like "It's *awfully* funny, isn't it?" and "I never expected to understand so much," Des still hadn't arrived. Win and Dawn had no option but to begin taking orders and serving them in double quick time, seeming at times to have four hands each, and needing six, and taking the next orders while giving change from the previous one and totting up prices in their heads and being at both ends of the bar at once. And when they collided over the red wines or the whiskeys, Win would mutter to Dawn: "Where is Des? He promised faithfully he'd come. There's much too many of them for the two of us to cope with. Where *is* Des?"

Chapter 7

RECEPTION

They didn't find Des until long after the play was over. As soon as the audience had been summoned by bell back to the courtyard, Win sent Dawn off with two trays of glasses, to pile them into the dishwasher in the kitchen. There wouldn't be time to do all of them by hand, she said, and she was right. The concert ended at nine-fifteen, and as the Town Hall was only five minutes away, it was not long before some members of the orchestra staying at the Saracen drifted in, and then soloists. Natalya had walked back with Singh. They had not been able to communicate very much, but since Singh was wrapped in a cloud of self-approbation brought on by a gaggle of critics, arts administrators, and early music enthusiasts who had fawned over him at Interval, and since even Natalya was quietly hugging herself at the warmth of her reception, they had been companionably quiet.

Siugh had gone straight to the rooms *en suite* that he shared with Brad, but they soon joined Natalya in the Shakespeare. Now they were both positively purring with delight, though Natalya thought she had never seen

Brad's hands flap more nervously. Singh had been offered a prestigious engagement for the next Bach Festival and had been urgently pressed to take the role of Idamante in a new Welsh National Opera production of *Idomeneo*. Natalya congratulated them but would have been more interested in offers that would display her own talents. After a time, she left them to their delighted self-absorption and watched the closing stages of the play from the window. The second half of the play was shorter, being mainly Deptford and whores and rollicking fun, but it ended with a great scene of reconciliation and matrimony, which was guaranteed to send audiences out with a warm glow. By five to ten it was all over, and the actors, with Jason, were receiving delighted acclamation from the audience. The great gates were opened, and critics scurried away to telephone in their reviews for the later editions. Then the Shakespeare was bustling once more.

"I suppose we can cope," said Win to Dawn, "since we did at Interval. There's not the same rush now. There's over an hour to closing time."

It was always pleasant at the Saracen after the play was over. Some of the actors, still in costume, usually mingled with the audience, as Peter Fortnum did now, though he confined his attentions to Natalya Radilova, going off with her into a corner and having a long and serious conversation. Constance Geary was in the Shakespeare, too, letting longtime admirers buy her drinks. Before long Krister Kroll arrived—the general public being admitted after the play was over—wanting to talk about the concert. He had changed into casuals and looked very handsome, but after trying to break into the rapt little duo of Mallory and Singh, he gave up and went over to join Peter and Natalya. He was welcome, because he was the sort of person who always was welcome.

In another corner Gillian, Ronnie Wimsett, and Jason Thark were going over the performance blow by blow. Gillian was just deciding that they were doing this mainly as a boost to Jason's ego, rather than with any thought of revising or strengthening the production, when a thought struck her.

"I say, the Great Australian Blight's not here. I'd have expected him to be worming his way around, calling Stanislavski to our attention or telling us to speak up and speak out."

"Probably got other fish to fry," said Ronnie Wimsett. "Some agreeable little piece of blackmail or something."

"I suppose it's too much to hope that he's had a heart attack while executing some particularly problematic yoga exercise?" hazarded Jason Thark.

Gillian suddenly noticed that Win Capper was collecting glasses and ashtrays at the next table, and she kicked the other two. When Win turned around, she smiled and said: "I'd have thought your husband would have been here, Mrs. Capper, to tell us how we'd done."

She had nothing against Win Capper, but the faint spark of malice in the last words was irresistible. It eluded Win Capper.

"I'd have thought he would've myself. I was expecting him at Interval, but he never showed. Rushed off our feet we were. I expect he's got something on."

"I expect *so*," said Gillian.

Win had spotted the great bulk of Frank, the commissionaire, standing proprietorially by the door of the bar.

"Frank, you seen Des?"

Frank's forehead creased. "Saw him during the first half, Mrs. C. He went in and watched the play for a bit."

"Haven't you seen him since then?"

"Only when he came out. He went into Reception, said he'd either be there or up in the flat if he was wanted. He said he might look in on the second half, but he didn't. He's not in Reception now. Want me to call up the stairs?"

Win considered. "No. Better not. He'll have something on. He hates being disturbed when he's got something on."

"I *bet* he does," muttered Ronnie Wimsett as Win moved away.

At eleven o'clock Win called "Time," and at ten past she flicked the light switch two or three times. The townspeople and festival-goers had drifted away, but the performers were reluctant for the evening to end.

"Don't they have any all-night bars in this place?" demanded Krister Kroll.

At the bar Win contemplated the second mountain of dirty glasses and ashtrays.

"It really is too much," she said to Dawn. "I think we should count this as a special night and leave everything till morning. I'll ring Des and tell him."

But when she dialed the flat number on the telephone behind the bar, she got no reply.

"But if he's not in the flat, where *is* he?" she said in bewilderment to Frank, who had just come into the bar again. "I just hope he's not *ill*—but Des is never ill. He's so conscious of health things."

"That sort's sometimes the first to go," said Frank with gloomy tactlessness. "Would you like me to go up and have a look."

"Oh, dear…Well, I think *I'd* better go. You know how Des is—But if he's not in the flat, I don't know where to look…"

She bustled off, distractedly poking at a stray strand of hair. Everyone left in the bar had been pushing back their chairs, preparatory to going to bed or continuing the parties in their rooms. Something made them wait. It *was* odd that Des had not been around after the show—*his* show, or so he had often seemed to believe. From his table in the corner with Natalya and Krister Kroll, Peter could see through the glass door of the Shakespeare Bar. He saw Win go out, saw her cross the hotel entrance lobby, saw her go around the reception desk and into the manager's room behind. Then he could see no more, but could only wait. It was not a long wait—less than a minute—before he heard clattering footsteps falling over themselves on the stairs and cries, cries that continued as Win stumbled through the manager's room and out into Reception, her face twisted in horror, her hands blood-stained.

"Oh! Oh, my God! He's dead! He's been killed! Frank! Frank! Call the doctor. No. Call the police. Someone's killed my Des!"

Chapter 8

THE MANAGER'S OFFICE

In the car from the Police Station, coming from the other side of town, Superintendent Iain Dundy gazed gloomily out over the dark, nearly deserted streets of Ketterick. He was a man in his mid-thirties, with a broken marriage behind him, a reputation for fairness, and a long fuse to his temper. He was already possessed by the conviction that on this case he was going to need it.

"I've always thought of myself as an unprejudiced man," he said apropos of nothing to Sergeant Nettles, who was driving. "I've never had any sort of a 'thing' against homosexuals, never hated blacks or Indians. Most of the Japanese I've met seemed perfectly charming, though I've never been able to understand a word they've said. I've had a holiday in Germany and quite like the people, and most of the American tourists we get here seem pleasanter than you're led to expect. I even once had a friend who was a Northern Ireland Protestant...But I do hate arty people. I admit it. I can't stand them. They touch a nerve in me. I've had a feeling ever since this festival started up that one day I was going to get stuck with a case chock-a-block full of arty people. And I wouldn't mind betting this is it!"

His expression became positively dyspeptic as the police car drew up outside the main entrance to the Saracen's Head.

It was difficult, the Saracen residents found, to know what to do after Win's spine-chilling reappearance. Of course, she had to be seen to first. While Frank made an imperative phone call to the police from the reception desk, Gillian helped Dawn, the stand-in barmaid, to get Win into the Shakespeare and settle her onto the sofa. But when Frank came back with a portentous expression on his face, as if the world's cares were now on his shoulders, and when he had announced that the police were on their way and had peremptorily forced on Win a stiff neat brandy, there really seemed nothing left for the rest of them to do. Actors do not commonly feel themselves *de trop*, but that was how they felt now. Win, after all, had never seemed particularly to take to their company, and she obviously would be more at ease with her own kind, whatever that was. She was moaning, "Oh, it was horrible," and crying intermittently, but she was calming down. To leave might seem like copping out, but to stay and gawp would surely be vulgar—since Sir Henry Irving, the British actor, has above all things eschewed vulgarity. They cleared their throats awkwardly and skulked off.

"We'll be in our rooms," said Jason, "if we should be wanted," and Frank nodded importantly.

That wasn't how it worked out, though. Singh certainly went to his room; he said to Brad that he wanted to see the late-night movie, which was *The Texas Chain-Saw Massacre*. Gillian went rather green at that, but Brad Mallory murmured fondly: "Oh—the young! They have such wonderful powers of recuperation." Though in fact Singh had given no sign of having anything to recuperate from. The rest of them seemed instinctively to cling together. The thought of solitary bedrooms was uninviting. They lingered in one of the large, open spaces on the first floor, which had a window looking out onto the High Street. From there, silent, they saw the police arrive—first the detectives, then a uniformed constable, who took up position outside the main entrance, then several more from the uniformed lower ranks. The actors had an odd sense of passing almost imperceptibly from one drama into another. This second one was certainly not going to be amusing.

"If only," said Ronnie Wimsett, "if only we knew exactly *when* he died."

"Why?" asked Gillian.

"Because, dear dumb cluck, if he died during the play and if he's up there in his flat, you must see that no one of us could have done it."

"I never considered for a moment that one of us could have," said Jason Thark. The silence that followed this was one of relief, as if Jason's position as producer gave him some sort of authority in police matters as well. That his statement was untrue, however, he immediately revealed by his next. "I suspect that we can narrow down the time much more closely than merely that of the duration of the play. Because when I was getting my drink after the show, poor old Win was wondering where Des was, and that girl from the dining room—Dawn is her name?—said rather sharply: 'It's no good him showing up now. It was during Interval that he was wanted and when he said he'd be here.' So I rather suspect that the police will find that he's been dead some time."

"Which will let us out," said Ronnie Wimsett.

"We-e-ell," began Gillian, but she was interrupted by footsteps on the stairs. And not just footsteps. The carrying voices of the Galloways were unmistakable.

"It was Des, dreadful Des," came Clarissa's voice.

"Are you quite sure?"

"I heard the commissionaire, or doorman, or whatever you call him, say it to the constable by the main entrance. 'His name is Capper, or was. Des Capper.' Unless he's gone out of his mind, the police are here because somebody's dead, and that somebody is Des Capper."

"Well, I'll be damned" came Carston's impeccably well-bred tones.

They emerged blinking from the stairwell: Clarissa, Carston, and Susan Fanshaw, who characteristically was saying nothing. When they had got their bearings, Clarissa stared triumphantly at the assembled cast of *The Chaste Apprentice of Bowe.*

"There! You see? Everyone's here and discussing it, aren't you, darlings?"

"We are," admitted Connie Geary. "But where have you been that you missed the fun?"

"Oh, my dear, such a miscalculation! I wouldn't have missed being first to hear of dreadful Desmond's death for the world if I'd known! But how could I? We went to the Webster."

"Why on earth did you do that?"

Clarissa had her audience and, as was her wont, immediately began acting a big scene, though it was a little enough matter she had to tell of.

"Well, darlings, after the play and the curtain calls—only there is no curtain, and I *do* find that awkward!—Carston and I changed, because the fact is we do feel it a *tin*y bit unprofessional to mingle with the dear old general public in costume—" She gestured round at Ronnie and Peter, still in their apprentice's costumes. "Call us old-fashioned if you like."

"Old-fashioned," said Gillian, and was rewarded with a dazzling reptilian smile.

"So when we were ready, we collected Susan Fanshaw, my husband's *sweet* little mistress, who had had a heavy evening seeing you'd all got your swords and cudgels with you and that your wimples and codpieces were straight, or whatever codpieces are supposed to be, and we went out into the yard, and there were *fans* waiting for us, still waiting after all that time…Well, we saw you all in the Shakespeare, and we thought we ought to *spread* ourselves around a bit so as to be fair, so we took the fans into the Webster and let them lavish on us the best hospitality their purses could buy. Poor dears, they loved it!"

Susan Fanshaw looked at Clarissa (from behind her) with an expression of the utmost contempt on her face. Clearly she had been embarrassed by their sponging. Carston did not notice the glance and took her hand absentmindedly.

"Anyway, the consequence was, you missed all the excitement," said Brad Mallory. "Win's announcement was a real Act One curtain, I can tell you."

"Darling, don't tor*ment* me! I would so have enjoyed it. Because the fact that he's been murdered—I take it, with all those police, murder is in question?—"

"Apparently," said Jason.

"—the fact that he's been murdered does seem a

singularly apt retribution for his grubby little interference into my private life."

"Don't say that to the police," said Carston, sighing.

"They might scent a whiff of megalomania. Or paranoia. It takes an odd kind of mind to find death an appropriate punishment for rummaging around in someone's drawers."

"Carston, of *course* I am not so stupid as to talk like that to the dear policemen. Naturally I shall tell them what an *int*eresting little man he was, with his homely medical advice and his en*tranc*ing accent and his *fasci*nating memories of the last days of the Raj. I shall say that in the short time we have been here I had come to number him amongst my *dear*est friends."

"Don't overdo it the other way either, Clarissa," said Jason in a tired voice. "The police are trained to smell rats." He added, rather insultingly: "And the last thing I need at this stage is to lose one of my leads."

"Fortunately I've always found the police to be charming and *most* respectful," said Clarissa, hardly hearing. "I've always got on famously with them."

"Don't I remember," said Carston.

"This is all getting way off the point," said Gillian. "When you came, we were trying to establish when he'd been murdered. We rather think it must have been before Interval."

"Before about eight-thirty, then?" asked Carston.

"That's it. Or a few minutes after. We were running ever so slightly late."

"And it must have been after—oh—seven-ten, seven-fifteen," contributed Carston.

"Oh?"

"Because he was standing at the back during the first

scene and into my bit in the second scene. I've got good long sight, and there's a moment when I peer into the audience, trying to see Sir Pecunius arriving from the Palace of Westminster. I saw him at the back then, and I saw him leave, which almost put me off my stride. So it was after that."

"Brilliant!" said Ronnie, rubbing his hands. "So we have a *terminus post quem* and a *terminus ante quem*. And they let all the actors out entirely. Because we'd have had to go through the kitchens, which had a card game going on in them, then through the dining room, which had most of the staff there, judging from their faces at the windows, then through the Shakespeare into the foyer. No way anyone could do that and then murder Des without being seen. Anyway, we were all behind the stage when we were not on it."

His words fell on an embarrassed silence. Gillian looked down at her hands and then dared to look up at Peter Fortnum. She found that Jason and Connie were looking at him too, and Natalya was looking at them and frowning in puzzlement.

"Well, not quite *all* the time," said Peter, brazening it out.

"Come along, let's go to bed," said Connie briskly. "They're going to want to question us in the morning. Let's leave the question of my gin till then. We'll go to bed and think things through."

And that was exactly what they did. Some of them had a great many things to think through.

While the actors and musicians had been chewing over things in the alcove, Superintendent Dundy had been sweating his way through some preliminary questioning of Mrs. Capper in the little manager's office behind the reception desk.

No, Mrs. Capper had said, she didn't mind talking. Would rather, really. Would rather go to bed knowing she'd got it over. And if she talked it through with him, perhaps the memory of poor Des lying there with the dagger between his shoulder blades would become less horribly vivid.

So talk she did, with Iain Dundy keeping her, at the start, on fairly neutral background topics.

"When did we come to Britain? Let's see, it was the time of the miners' strike—not the last one, the one before that. Seventy-four, was it? I remember because there was no electricity most of the time, and lots of the industries were shut down, and the shops, and I wanted to go home after I'd been here a couple of days, I can tell you."

"Home?"

"New South Wales. Des was manager of a very nice hotel in Dubbo. I wish we'd never left. People don't go sticking knives into each other in Dubbo."

Dundy let pass this romanticization of her past. "Why did you leave?" he asked.

"Just chance, really. There was this English hotelier stayed with us, got pally with Des—everyone got on well with Des—and offered us a job. Des thought if we didn't go then, we never would, though it wouldn't have broken my heart if we never had. This was back in—oh, seventy-three, it must have been. So eventually we came over, and Des became bar manager of this big hotel in Bournemouth. Then it was manager of the Excelsior in Carlisle, then here. All of them hotels in the Beaumont chain. Des was very pleased to get Ketterick. It's what he called a prestige hotel in the group, and it gave him a bit of a stake in this festival that's going on now."

"You weren't so pleased?"

Win Capper shrugged. "Drinkers are pretty much alike wherever you are, that's what I say. And the people who go on about what a lovely hotel it is don't think of the amount of walking that's involved!"

"But what about your husband? Had he enjoyed his time since you both came here?"

"Oh, yes. Happy as a lamb with two tails. All this airy-fairy arty stuff was meat and drink to him. But of course Des was a very well-read man."

"And he got on well with people?"

"Oh, yes! Des was always good chums with people right from the word go."

"Why was that?"

"Well, he never put on airs. He was always chatty and always had an appropriate word for everybody. As I say, he knew an awful lot. He had an inquiring mind."

Iain Dundy wondered whether an inquiring mind was really likely to make a hotel manager popular. Des Capper was dead, after all. Perhaps he had pursued his inquiries in foolish or dangerous directions. He said: "You mean he was interested in everyone?"

"Well, I meant more that he knew what everybody was interested in, so he was on their wavelength and could talk with them. Like about acting and singing with this lot now. He could give them tips, little bits of advice. And I think he was very useful on the festival committee. He'd really wised himself up on the play they're doing, and he was starting to read up about this opera with the silly title. He said he had to be clued up, so he could discuss with the people staying here. He was very thorough, was Des. And a walking encyclopedia sometimes!"

More like a barroom philosopher, Dundy guessed, and a know-all to boot. Des sounded quite unbearable.

"So what exactly happened tonight?" he asked.

"Oh, Lord…I wish I could forget it…We opened at six, but just for members of the audience, because we don't open to members of the public until after the play's over. We were quite busy. I was behind the bar, and Des was going around talking to people in the Shakespeare, as he usually did. I had to call him over to help me, and I told him we wouldn't be able to cope at Interval time without him. He said he'd come. Then of course the audience started drifting out into the yard to take their seats, and Des knocked off. That was the last I saw of him until—"

"Did he say where he was going?"

"He said he might go and watch the play for a bit from the back. Frank—that's the doorman—says that's what he did. Dawn and I were busy in the bar, so I didn't think about him until he didn't turn up at Interval."

"You and this other barmaid—Dawn is it?"

"Yes. She's one of the waitresses, and very capable."

"You were together in the Shakespeare Bar the whole time until Interval?"

If Win Capper understood why he was asking this, she gave no sign. She just answered obediently, as if she were a child in class answering by rote.

"Dawn went to fetch the snacks from the kitchen. That took three or four minutes, I should think. Otherwise we were together the whole time."

"And you had to cope together at Interval?"

"That's right. We were so rushed that I didn't have time to ring around for Des."

"And after the Interval you didn't get worried?"

"I knew he would have come if he could." She dabbed at her eyes, which were very full. "I didn't *think*. How could I? And I knew we could cope after the show, because most people go straight off home. Dawn told me that; she'd helped out previous years. Anyway, after the Interval we got everything shipshape again and got the glasses washed, and then, when the concert finished, people started coming in again."

"When was that?"

"Twenty, twenty-five past nine. The Town Hall's only five minutes away, and some of the residents came straight back here. Our Interval had finished a bit before nine—ten or five to. Then, of course, when the play ended, towards ten, we filled up quite considerably."

"Tell me about finding him."

"Oh, my God, do I have to? You've seen—" She swallowed at the memory.

"Try to do it quite objectively, as if it were someone else involved, someone else's body."

She looked up at him as if hardly understanding, but then she swallowed again and tried.

"We were quite busy until just after eleven, but after I'd called 'Time' I realized I hadn't seen Des since before seven. And that wasn't right. He'd have wanted to go round the Shakespeare and talk to people after the play, see how they thought it had gone. I wasn't exactly *worried*, because he could have been in the Webster or the Massinger, but the Shakespeare is very much *his* bar and the easiest to get to from Reception and the flat. And then Frank said he hadn't seen him since soon after the play started. That didn't seem right, either. So I rang the flat, and there was no reply, and then I *did* start to wonder."

"Did your husband have any history of illness?"

"No, always fit as a fiddle. Like I said, he had this thing about health and lots of little tips about how to keep in shape. He read up on it you know…Still, he is over sixty…*Was*…So you do think about heart attacks…Anyway, I went to the manager's office, and he wasn't there, and I opened the door that leads up to the flat and called—"

"Was the door unlocked?"

"Yes. It usually was, except at night. So I went up the stairs and opened the door into our lounge, and—well, there he was. You couldn't not see him."

"Was the body exactly as it is now? Did you disturb it in any way?"

"No. Or not much. You see, I screamed, and then I knelt down and looked at his face, so I maybe touched his shoulders. But I know a dead body when I see one. And there was the knife between his shoulders—"

"You recognized the knife?"

"Oh, yes, it was a knife that Des brought back from India years ago. Had it before we were married. It was always on the little table by the sofa."

"Had you or your husband ever entertained any of the present festival guests at the hotel in your private flat?"

"Not that I know of. Why would we?"

Why indeed? Dundy thought.

"Did you notice whether anything else had been disturbed in the flat?"

"No, I just got up and...ran downstairs. Screaming. It was so horrible."

Iain Dundy looked at his watch. "I think that's all we need from you tonight, Mrs. Capper. Have you got anything to make you sleep?"

"Not personal. Des didn't approve of things like that. But there'll be something around somewhere in case one of the hotel guests asked for it."

"Then I suggest you take it. You'll be able to use one of the hotel rooms to sleep in, won't you? Oh—one last question: Did your husband, to your knowledge, have any enemies?"

She looked at him, wide-eyed.

"Oh, no. Des didn't have an enemy in the world. Anyone'll tell you the same."

He jumped up and opened the door for her, and she walked across the foyer to where Dawn was waiting for her by the door into the Shakespeare. At the sight of a friend and female sympathy, Win tottered a little as she walked and then crumpled into her arms, to be led inside.

"Excuse me, sir."

Dundy swung round and saw that there was a young man standing talking to the constable at the main entrance. He had an air of fledgling copper about him, but he wasn't a policeman Dundy knew. This he was sure of because he was black, and black policemen were rare enough to notice. When he raised his eyebrows, the young man came over.

"They sent me from the station, sir. I'm Metropolitan CID, but I was there visiting a mate from training days. They thought I might be useful because I was in the audience tonight."

"Here, for the play?"

"That's right, sir."

"You might well be useful. Are you free at the moment?"

"Free for the next forty-eight hours." He held out his hand. "I'm Peace, sir. Charlie Peace."

Chapter 9

THE HOTEL STAFF

"I don't know how much help I can be," said Charlie Peace as Dundy gestured him to the vacant armchair in the small office. "The bloke on the door says he was killed in the hotel here."

"That's right."

"I can't say I registered much from inside the hotel while the play was going on. Women collecting up glasses in the bar, staff watching the play from the dining room—not much more than that."

"Why were you at the play?"

"Came with a girlfr—Well, a girl. Student at London University. She asked me along, and I came to see if she was really interested or whether it was the okay thing these days for girl students to have a black boyfriend."

"And which was it?"

"We said polite farewells at the gate." Charlie's mouth expanded suddenly into a great, generous grin. "Plenty more where that came from."

"But you've got a clear idea of the play itself?"

"Oh, yes. It wasn't half bad, really, and one or two

good laughs. Oh, I remember what went on onstage. It's what went on behind the stage that you'll be interested in, won't it, sir?"

Dundy sighed. "It will. Most of that will have to wait till tomorrow, though. Shall we contact the Yard and see if we can use you for a couple of days? Then you might get days off in lieu."

"If you could," said Charlie. "Days off have been pretty scarce as long as the football season's lasted. Are you going to be doing anything more tonight, sir?"

"Well, there was one thing…Did you notice that doorman chappie, Nettles?"

"Oh, yes, sir. Know him by sight. Probably even exchanged a few words, back in the days when I was on the beat."

"My guess from the look of him is that beneath that old-soldier exterior there lurks a leaky-mouthed individual who'd tell you his life story for the price of a pint."

"I think that's probably true, sir. The bloke on the door says he's already had his war memoirs."

"He didn't give him his boss's life story as well, did he?"

"Afraid not. But he did say the place had gone to the dogs since he took over."

"Right. That sounds like an antidote to Mrs. Capper's 'not an enemy in the world' delusions. Let's have him in now."

✿ ✿ ✿

"Is that what she said?" asked Frank, the doorman, shooting a cynical smile across the manager's desk at Iain Dundy and taking in Nettles and Charlie as he licked his lips in anticipation. "Life and soul of the Shakespeare, popular with all and sundry?"

"That's pretty much what she told me," said Dundy, looking straight at him.

"Balls," said Frank succinctly. His mouth was still working with relish at the prospect of character assassination ahead, and there was a glint in his old eyes. "Balls with the best of intentions, I don't doubt. I'm sure she believed every blessed word she spoke. But it's balls nonetheless."

"Not popular?"

"About as welcome as the death-watch beetle." Frank expanded in his chair in the manager's office. This was the life. This was something to take home to the missus. A murder investigation and him in on the ground floor. Key witness, in fact, by reason of his position outside the main entrance. *And* he could tell them a thing or two about the hotel, the superintendent would find, a thing or two that he wouldn't hear from anyone else. There wasn't much that had escaped him in the last week or two.

Iain Dundy looked at Frank skeptically: his big body expanding with self-importance, his furry mustache twitching with relish at the idea of being part of a murder inquiry. He had been through the events of the evening with him, when he had last seen Des, and so on, and that had been moderately satisfactory. Now he was getting on to the nitty-gritty, which was hearsay and conjecture, and all the more enjoyable to Frank for that. He'll tell me everything, thought Dundy, but will that everything be right? He looks like the sort of man who turns suggestions into conjecture and conjecture into fact in the twinkling of an eye. Basically a stupid man but possibly to be trusted on the things he knows best. And he must have come to know Des Capper pretty well.

"Mind you," Frank resumed, "fair's fair. He came after poor old Arthur Bradley—Know Arthur, did you? Most everyone did hereabouts. Him being so popular and the perfect gent, it would have been difficult for anyone coming after. This one no sooner showed his nose and everyone was asking why the devil he'd been appointed."

"You mean, if he was unpopular in the Saracen, it wasn't altogether his fault?"

Frank scratched his ear in puzzlement. "No, I don't altogether mean that. What I suppose I'm trying to say is that no one could have been really popular, but he sank plumb to the bottom of the charts. And that was because of what he did and the sort of man he was."

"Maybe you'd better explain," suggested Dundy.

And explain Frank did. Explained Des's manner—the oozing, oleaginous manner that hid the desire to dominate. Explained his know-all ways that made him believe he could pronounce and advise on all subjects under the sun. Explained that on his daily rounds as manager of the hotel he made it his business to gain knowledge of his guests rather than to minister to their comfort. And Frank went further. He made it clear that if it struck Des's fancy to use his knowledge, gain a covert pleasure by flaunting it, then that is exactly what he would do.

"To take a case in point," Frank concluded, still expressing the utmost pleasure in his narration by the whole set of his body. "This happened several weeks ago, but I actually saw it, and I can vouch for it. There was this bloke, late middle-aged, who'd been here before with this dolly-bird, who he'd signed in as *Mrs.* Williams, or whatever it was. This time he had a middle-aged lady, one on the sour side, or that was how she looked, and she was also Mrs. Williams, obviously the real one. He was a fool to do it, but there you are—some people *are* fools. Now, dinnertime it was, and I had to deliver a telephone message to the next table, so I saw this as it happened. Des Capper was doing his rounds—the headwaiter does *not* like him doing it in the dining room, but he hadn't a hope in hell of stopping him—and he went up to the Williams table, obviously singling it out, and with his usual dripping-oil manner he said: 'Good evening, Mrs. Williams. Everything to your satisfaction, is it? This is the first time we've had the pleasure of welcoming you to the Saracen, I think?' And after the usual courtesies, he turns to her husband, and he says:

'*Mr.* Williams, on the other hand, we have seen before. Though that time, if I remember rightly, you were on your own, weren't you, sir?' And he puts his hand on the man's shoulder and applies a bit of pressure."

"Ouch!" said Iain Dundy.

"It was *daft*, that's what it was. One way to make sure that bloke was never again seen at the Saracen with or without fancy woman. There's hotels where a man like that knows he's safe, and there's others, and Des Capper had put us into the second category with a vengeance. But you see the sort of man he was, don't you? He couldn't resist that little display of—what shall I call it?—intimate knowledge, power over the man."

"And I suppose that at festival time there were plenty of things going on in the hotel that Mr. Capper could feed on?"

"Was there ever! *I* get a kick out of the goings-on at festival time, I can tell you. So you can guess what Des Capper was like. Went poking his nose in everything, giving advice here, a little bit of reminiscence there, and sniffing out intimate secrets all over the shop!"

"Which was not popular with the guests, I imagine?"

"They were getting up a petition, that I *do* know."

"A petition?"

"To get a change of manager by next year. Des unsuitable in view of the central position of the Saracen in the events of the Ketterick festival—that kind of thing."

"Hmmm. Interesting. Have you any idea what kinds of thing Capper had found out in these nosings around?"

"Ah—there you may find Win knows more than I do." He winked. "Pillow talk. Though mostly when he spoke to her it was to give orders. As far as him and me were concerned, we didn't swap information. I like to know what's going on as much as the next man, but with me it's just a case of 'That's the way the world goes.' With him it was something more…something nasty. Mind you, as often as not he'd know I knew, and I'd know he knew, if you get me. As in the case of Mr. Gottlieb—I beg his pardon: Herr Gottlieb."

Iain Dundy sighed. At last we must be coming to the arty ones, he thought. "And who is Mr. Gottlieb?"

"Some kind of musician. Conductor, I think. Travels around with a couple of heavies. And this is the grubby bit, which is what Des enjoyed most, because he really had a nose for the grubby: They pimp for him from among his fans. It's almost like them pop stars back in the sixties. He had one of the little groupies visiting him tonight, and Des commented on it when he came back from watching the play."

"So there were visitors to the hotel during the first half of the play?"

"Just the one. Just her. Between her going and Mr. Mallory coming back from the concert, there was nobody."

"Capper was interested in the girl, was he?"

"You bet. He was interested in anything connected with Gottlieb. Probably goes back to the war or something, though he always says he was in India and the Far East. Mind you, so far as I can see, everybody seems to hate Gottlieb. But with Des it seemed to have a special edge."

"But he never talked it over with you or told you why?"

"No, he just winked when I told him about the girl."

"Anyone else he was interested in?"

"Oh, everyone. His little antennae were always a-twitch. But not everyone gave him the sort of raw material he was interested in. There were the Galloways, of course—"

"Ah, *them* I've heard of," said Dundy. "May even have seen them on tour or on television. Definitely a couple, aren't they? Melissa is her name? And—"

"Clarissa and Carston. Yes, they act as a team, as often as not, and they were here a couple of years ago, when they created the same sort of brouhaha. They *act* as a team, but they don't act like a team, if you get my meaning, sir. Not offstage. She's sleeping with the producer, and he's sleeping with an assistant stage manager, and everyone has to put up with a running commentary on the whole business from dawn to dusk, which is part of some sort of nonstop row they're having."

"A row about that?"

"I don't think so. No, according to the room maid they're completely open about that. But they spend their time sniping at each other nonetheless, and they give the impression that's as much habit as anything else."

"Maybe it is. On the other hand, there could be a specific reason, and Capper could somehow have got wind of it.

Anything else?"

"One of the older actresses drinks. Who doesn't these days? A fair bit of A sleeping with B. Not all that interesting. Then there's something interesting happening around the Russian lady."

"Oh?"

"Something hush-hush."

"Do you think she wants to defect?"

"Maybe. I expect that's probably it. But if so, she's a long time about it. What's to stop her defecting now if she wants to? Anyway, there's something going on between her and one of the younger actors. Peter Fortnum, his name is, and he speaks Russki. Of course, it could be just good old-fashioned sex, but it looks like something more, *too*. If she's wanting to defect, I'd have thought Mr. Mallory would be in on it, too, but though this Fortnum is always making hush-hush phone calls and going to and fro with messages, I haven't noticed that Mr. Mallory is involved in any way."

"You mentioned Mallory before. Who exactly is he—and what?"

"A poncy agent. He acts for the Russian lady and for a superponcy Indian boy who apparently sings with that choirboy's voice I can't stand. He was at the concert tonight, of course."

"But did you say he came back at Interval time?"

"That's right. He said he left at the *concert* Interval, and he got back to the Saracen sometime before *our*

Interval here. Around eight-fifteen, I'd say. He'd heard Singh—that's the name of his poncy Indian boyfriend, if you'll believe it—do his bit and came away. 'Singh sang divinely,' he said. That was all he was interested in."

"So the only outsider who came into the hotel during the first half of the performance—say, from seven to about eight-thirty—was the girl for this German conductor?"

"That's right. Austrian, I think he is, if you're getting technical."

"Otherwise there was Des Capper coming out to watch the play from the courtyard and then going back in again?"

"That's right. And going on about how he was going to serve in the bar at Interval, as if it was the height of bloody condescension on his part to serve in his own pub."

"And then just Mr. Mallory?"

"Right again."

"Now, you were talking, I know. Can you really be quite sure that no one could have got past you?"

"Sure and doubly sure. Bob and I talk every year during the play, but both of us keep our eyes open. It's our job to stop gate-crashers, and we do."

"What about the other entrances?"

"Well, obviously there are other entrances on a normal day. Each of the three bars has one, for instance, and there are doors into the kitchens. But naturally, when the play is on, you can only keep open manned entrances, and that means the one in the central gate. All the others are locked, and I watch the one into the hotel and Reception."

"That was the regular procedure each year, was it? Not something Mr. Capper had organized?"

"No, no, I've been doing it for years now. And as I say, generally me and Bob at the ticket gate meet halfway and have a bit of a natter, because we can't watch the play even if we'd wanted to, which we don't. But we keep a sharp eye on our entrances. You couldn't have it getting around that there were ways of slipping into the plays without buying a ticket."

"Well, if that's true, it does narrow the field a bit. And the field could do with some narrowing." Iain Dundy sighed and looked round at Nettles and Charlie, sitting quiet and respectful in the background. That young Peace looked as if he was following well. He was on the ball and was going to be of help. Dundy looked at him as he said:

"Anything else, I wonder?"

Charlie cleared his throat. "Just one thing, sir. I was here with a girl for the performance, as you know—"

"That's right," put in Frank. "Saw you going in."

Charlie smiled at him ferociously, as if daring him to voice the thoughts that had gone through his mind at the time. "Well, I thought you should know that we went into the Shakespeare Bar at Interval, and the door out to the street *was* locked, because we thought of going outside to get some air. At the time I wondered about fire risk. As it was, we had to go out into the courtyard again, which was very crowded, what with the seats and all the people."

"Right," said Iain Dundy. "So that confirms what has just been said."

"That's right, sir. There was just a question in my mind about the key. It wasn't in the door, of course, or we could just have turned it and gone out. I wondered who had it."

"It would be Mrs. Capper," said Frank promptly. "And the barmen in the other bars would have had theirs with them, too, while the play was going on. I think it's the headwaiter who sees to the back kitchen door. The drill was that they would open up just as the performance was ending."

"Right."

"The chief fire officer has okayed the arrangement," said Frank self-importantly. "The fact is, we can get the big gates open in a matter of thirty seconds, so the major part of the audience would be out in the twinkling of an eye. The balconies are not high, and there are rope ladders on every one."

Dundy nodded. "Well, I think that's it—for the moment only, of course. I'll want to check up on details later. I wonder if that girl Dawn is still around. If she is, maybe I could just tie up a few loose ends with her before everyone goes off to bed."

"She was getting poor old Win Capper off to sleep," said Frank. "She's a very conscientious girl. She may have waited to see if she was wanted."

And she had. She had started cleaning up the Shakespeare, but one of the constables had said she'd better not do that in case there was anything there that might be important in the way of evidence. So she had sunk down into a chair in the foyer and lit a cigarette. She was a smart girl, with normally dancing eyes and a humorous expression. Now she was tired to the point of exhaustion, but she tried to pull herself together enough to answer Dundy's questions.

"The last time I saw Mr. Capper? Let me see, that

would be before the play started. Mrs. Capper had got him to help behind the bar. Not that he was much help, I imagine—all talk and very little action."

"You didn't like him?"

"Nobody did," said Dawn blithely, with the confidence born of a feeling that no one was likely to accuse her of murdering her boss. "I don't want to speak ill of the dead, but it doesn't do to tell lies about them, either, does it? He was damn-all use about the place, and that's a fact. Win did all the work, and she was nothing better than his slave."

"Nevertheless, Mrs. Capper got her husband to promise that he'd be there to help at Interval?"

"That's right. I came in just as they were talking about it, so I overheard. He was trying to wriggle out of it: 'You'll have Dawn to help you.' As if two was enough when they're crowded five or six deep waving five-pound notes at you! But he hated *serving*. He liked swanning around—that was all *he* was good for."

"And as it turned out, Mrs. Capper had only you for help, and you were with her all evening?"

"Yes, as it turned out. We coped at Interval. In point of fact, if you've got a third who doesn't do much but get in the way, he's more of a hindrance than a help. And Win had got a lot of glasses poured out in readiness while the first part was going on. So it was hectic, but we managed."

"But you *were* with Mrs. Capper all evening?"

Under Iain Dundy's calm, clear gaze, Dawn faltered as she understood what he was getting at.

"What you're saying," she muttered, "is that in this sort of case it's always the husband or wife who's suspected first. Though in fact Win thought Des was God's gift, poor cow."

"I'm not *saying* anything. I'm just trying to get at times."

"Yes, well—I filled the dishwasher in the kitchens with glasses in the second half. There were just too many to do in clear water in the bar, like Win normally would. That took me—what?—ten minutes."

"And in the first half?"

"I just fetched the snacks...They were something a bit special, a sort of free extra because it was the first night. There was a bit of balancing plates on the tray and that, but it couldn't have taken me more than five minutes. Less, if anything."

Iain Dundy gave a meaningful look at the other policemen that said, Five minutes would be enough. But Dawn, under inquisition, had regained some of her perkiness, and she noticed the look. She said, smiling sweetly: "And when I came back, Win had poured out drinks for Interval, like I said. While I'd been away, she'd done about fifteen white wines, about ten reds, and the same number of whiskeys and gins. You try doing that in five minutes and killing your husband!"

"Couldn't they have been done before you came on the scene?"

"Where would she have kept them? The white wines would have to have been kept in the fridge. I was in and out of the fridge during the first half of the play, getting ice and whatnot. There were no ready-poured glasses of white wine there; that I can tell you for sure."

Charlie cleared his throat. "Excuse me, sir," he said. "My girl had white wine at Interval. First thing she said when she sipped it was 'Lovely and cool!'"

Charlie's imitation of upper-class girlhood was perfect. Superintendent Dundy sat looking gloomily ahead of him. To Sergeant Nettles his expression said as clearly as words: It's the arty types we're going to be stuck with.

Finally he shifted in his chair and turned to Dawn with a smile. "Thank you, love. That'll be all for tonight. I think we ought all to go home and get an hour or two's kip."

Chapter 10

THE DINING ROOM

The headwaiter supervised breakfast next morning. This was not something that he did very often, but he did it the day after Des's murder. He had heard about the killing the night before, of course, as he and his staff were waiting for the last of the supper-takers to leave. Dawn had been the first to bring the news, and further snippets of information had been gleaned (by guile) from the many policemen infesting the Saracen's Head. The kitchen and dining-room staff had been thunderstruck and hadn't enjoyed anything so much in years. They had quite lost the desire to get rid of the eaters and go home to bed. In fact, they had related the news to favored eaters with varying degrees of subtlety. ("I'm sorry the service has been a bit erratic tonight, but you see, the manager's just been murdered.") The headwaiter participated in all their contradictory emotions, though on a loftier plane, of course, and he had made do with a very few hours' sleep in order to be at the Saracen early, apparently to ensure that the dining room's high standards of food and service were in no way compromised by the untoward little incident of the night before.

Incidentally, he also intended to be the first to inform the headquarters of the Beaumont hotel chain. It is in the nature of headwaiters that they like to be the first with news, however hushed, regretful, or reverent the tone of voice in which they choose to broadcast it.

Thus, when the various members of the cast and other residents of the hotel came down severally to breakfast, they found eggs scrambled to a nicety, kippers beautifully frizzled, the traditional fry-up traditionally fried up. What was different was the atmosphere. They all dallied over their breakfasts for a start, hoping that someone else would come down with a new theory they had thought up in the long watches. All the play people sat at adjacent tables (not something they normally did) and exchanged intimacies and abrasions across the gaps, while the orchestral players and odds and ends sat as near them as they decently could and listened unashamedly, as did the unusually attentive waitresses, who fussed unconscionably around the tables in the hope of picking up something new.

"The point is," said Jason Thark, still in the magisterial mood of the night before, "that it would be quite impossible for any of us to go through the dining room here without being seen. Let alone the kitchen, let alone the Shakespeare Bar, but the dining room would have been quite impossible. And we would have had to go through all three to get to the stairs that would have taken us up to the first floor. No—Ronnie was quite right: We're out of it."

"There was just one thing," said Ronnie, "something I've been thinking over during the night. When I was playing onstage, I was conscious of faces in the windows of the dining room watching the play...*Were* you?" he asked, swiveling round in his chair and transfixing the waitress, who was dawdling round with a toast rack in her hand as an excuse. She blushed.

"Well, some of us was watching."

"Never all of you?"

"No. Some of us watched some of the time. But you couldn't hear, not through the window, so you couldn't follow what was going on, though it looked a good laugh and you had us splitting our sides, sir."

"But some of you didn't watch at all?"

"No, sir."

"And where were the ones who were not at the window?"

"They were around the table by the door into the kitchen having a bit of a giggle and a gossip, sir."

Ronnie leaned back in his chair, satisfied.

"So I was right. Nobody could have got past."

"There was also some poker playing in the kitchen," volunteered the waitress, unwilling to lose the limelight now that she was used to it.

"Right. Them we could see from our part of the kitchen. I admit that they most probably wouldn't have noticed if anyone from the cast had tried to sneak past. But the gag—Sorry, collection of staff by the door into the kitchen would certainly have noticed anyone, wouldn't you?"

"Well, I expect so, sir. We did see this gentleman"— she gestured at Peter Fortnum—"go through and then go back again. Not that it meant anything, I'm sure."

She retreated rather suddenly from the table, as if she had all but accused Peter of murder. She left some embarrassment behind her as well, though not in Jason

Thark, who was impervious to any such human emotion.

"You see? She noticed. *One* of them would certainly have noticed if our murderer had tried to go that way. And apart from Peter, who was not to know that Connie would run out of gin, so I see no significance in his trip, nobody did."

For one moment this made everyone feel better. For only a moment.

"Oh, *come*," said Clarissa Galloway, putting back on her plate a delicate triangle of toast. "I really wouldn't have expected you to be so deficient in logic, Jason, my pet. For a start, Peter could have made sure Connie would run out by nicking a half from her bag. She said, if you remember, that she had never forgotten to have one there in reserve before. Secondly, he could have been intending to use some other excuse but seized on this when he heard Connie's laments. Of course, Peter *dar*ling, I'm not saying that any such thing happened, merely that we must, above all things, remain *log*ical, because we can be sure the police will."

"I quite understand," said Peter, tight-lipped.

As soon as he saw it was nine o'clock, the headwaiter ceased supervising the mundane business of distributing breakfast goodies and slipped into his little office in the corner of the kitchens. Somebody would now be in at the head office.

The Beaumont chain had hotels from Aberdeen to Bodmin and from the sublime to the disgusting. Its headquarters was in Kensington, and when the headwaiter made it clear that this was a matter of the utmost urgency, he was put through without further ado to the managing director's office.

"He'll not be in until ten or so," said the great man's secretary. "He's been at Brighton with his son—he's a spastic and takes a lot of looking after. Where did you say you were speaking from?"

"The Saracen's Head, in Ketterick."

"Alt, yes. One of the jewels in our crown."

"Precisely."

"Haven't you got that festival thing on there at the moment? I hope it's not causing any problems."

"No, or not directly. It's the manager. Mr. Capper..."

"Ye-es?" Did the headwaiter detect an note of wariness, or at least of circumspection?

"He's dead. Murdered."

"Good God! Have you called the police?"

The headwaiter raised his eyebrows to heaven. "It happened last night. Of course, the police have been here since then. That's all taken care of."

"I shall inform the managing director the moment he comes in. He'll be most upset. He knew Mr. Capper personally. And he won't like all the publicity there'll be. It will clash horribly with the Saracen Head's image."

It was the headwaiter's opportunity, the reason he had been so keen to relay the news. His voice took on tones of the most magisterial: "If you will allow me to say so, the whole Capper appointment clashed with the image."

"Ah..." There was silence at the other end, as if the secretary were not used to being taken down a peg or two by employees from the suburbs. "You thought so?"

"I would say the whole hotel thought so."

"As far as this office was aware, he was doing an

excellent job. He rang up last night, you know, to say that the play was going well. The duty man left a note for the managing director. He was first-rate like that, at keeping in touch. He must have been murdered after that."

"He must indeed. At what time did Mr. Capper make this phone call to your duty man?"

"The note is dated seven-thirty."

"I shall certainly inform the investigating officer."

"I hardly think—Is that necessary? Do we really want to involve Head office? Well, you must use your dis*cre*tion..."

"The main thing now is," interrupted the headwaiter, who had every intention of following his conscience and doing his duty as a citizen, "that we get a temporary manager as soon as possible. You do have qualified people who are between assignments, I suppose?"

"Oh, yes. Of course."

"The play isn't on tonight. It's the first night of the opera. After that the play runs every night of the festival except Sunday. It's essential we have somebody here by tomorrow. And preferably someone who could learn the ropes tonight."

"It's a tall order. But I'll list the possibilities and show them to the M.D. as soon as he gets in. I suppose Mrs. Capper isn't in a condition to—"

"Mrs. Capper is not the managing type, and by all accounts she is in no condition at the moment to do anything. It would hardly be seemly in any case even to have her helping behind the bar, whatever her mental state."

"No. No, of course not. Well, I'll try and get a lightning decision and ring you as soon as I have any news. Meanwhile, soldier on, eh?"

❄ ❄ ❄

The discussion was continuing in the dining room. Breakfast had never taken so long, but the kitchen staff was not complaining. The waitresses were picking up an unending stream of fact, conjecture, innuendo, and downright falsehood, and they were regaling it to the cooks, who were putting their own interpretations on them. ("You mark my words!" the head cook kept saying after each particularly bizarre leap of the imagination.) Before long, they all felt, they would be ready to make an arrest, even if the police were not.

"Right," Ronnie Wimsett was saying. "Peter's absence is not in dispute. He went to get gin for Connie. We all find it pretty impossible to get to our own rooms— *still,* after a fortnight here—so it's not surprising that he found it difficult to get to Connie's."

Peter, and Natalya, too, sat stewing over their tea, looking straight in front of them.

"The question is, could any of the rest of us do it? Now, to my mind, going through on the Webster and Massinger side of the hotel is simply out. For one reason, at some stage you would have to come *out*—either into the courtyard or into the street. In the courtyard you have audience who would see you, including twelve standing-room customers at the back, by the main gates, whose vision you would have to cross. On the other hand, if you go out into the street, you still have to get back in past hawk-eyed Frank on the main entrance. Impossible— right? That leaves the route via the kitchens and the Shakespeare, which is inconceivable for reasons we've already gone into. So all in all—apart from Peter, and sorry about that, old chap—there simply seems no way any of us *could* have done it."

There was silence after this, though one or two, notably Susan Fanshaw, looked unhappy. Indeed, she started to speak but cast a half look in the direction of Carston Galloway and cut the sound short in her throat.

"Well, that settles it," cooed Clarissa. "We'll explain it to that rather *mel*ancholy-looking policeman, and it will leave him free to direct his attentions elsewhere."

"After all," said Ronnie Wimsett, "we've been here for a couple of weeks or so, but Capper's been manager for months. Who knows what backs he's put up in his time?"

"The main thing is," said Carston, pushing back his chair and making to get up, "that we're all in the clear and can now get on with our business."

Brad Mallory's drawl broke unnervingly into the general euphoria. "Anyone would think," he said, "that the Saracen's Head was a one-story building."

He was sitting slightly apart, at a table for two, which Singh had just left. There was silence for a moment after his words, but then Ronnie Wimsett broke into it confidently:

"No, no, old chap. I've thought of that. To get to the stairs in the foyer outside the Shakespeare you still have to go through the kitchens, dining room, and the bar itself. And on the other side the stairs are between the Massinger and the Webster and you'd have to go through the one and could be seen from the other. No, that doesn't wash."

"Brad doesn't relish his position," said Clarissa in serpentine tones, "of being one of the few actually in the *hotel* part of the Saracen at the time of the killing."

Brad's smile in return revealed that he was hardly to be outdone in the friendly-snake department.

"Quite true if Des was killed after eight-fifteen. Yes, I could in fact have returned from the concert and gone straight upstairs and killed him. In *fact,* I went to my room, but I could just as easily have gone along to his flat. But what if he was already dead by eight-fifteen?"

Clarissa shrugged. "So what? It leaves us exactly where we were. Apart from young Peter, none of us could have gone through to the front part of the hotel."

Bradford Mallory, no less than Clarissa, could relish a big moment. "I seem to remember," he said, almost dreamily, "from one of my visits to your delightful play in rehearsal, a moment...a line—what was it? 'What mean these sudden broils so near my doors?' Something like that!"

"'Have you not other places but my house, to vent the spleen of your disordered bloods?'" went on Gillian Soames, as if this were something she had been itching to bring up for hours.

"I know what you're going to say," said Clarissa Galloway with all the considerable force at her disposal. She had put her hand over the breakfast table and covered her husband's in a display of solidarity. It was a revealing gesture, which suggested that their instinct was to thaw together at moments of crisis. She also revealed that this was something they had discussed overnight. Brad Mallory ignored her and went on in his dreamy fashion.

"It was, if I remember, a speech of Ralph Greatheart, at night, quieting the riotous behavior of the apprentices...and appearing to them in his nightshirt...appearing—and this is the point—*above,* on what we may call the upper stage. In fact, appearing on that part of the balcony over the center of the stage. Is that not right, Miss Fanshaw?"

"Yes," said Susan, tight-lipped.

"And my impression is that this scene occurs—what?—about an hour into the play?"

"Something like that," agreed Susan.

"And that with Ralph Greatheart on the balcony there is his stage wife and his daughter Alice—dear Gillian."

"Right," agreed Gillian.

"And did you, Miss Fanshaw, accompany them to the first floor to see that all was well?"

"No, I checked costumes and props at the bottom of the staircase as they all went up."

"The staircase," said Brad.

"I went up," said Jason Thark, hurriedly, before anyone else could mention it. "It was a tricky scene, and I went and stood in the bedroom behind."

"That's right," said Carston, "and you—" He shut up suddenly.

"I think, you know," said Brad, "that the police had better look into that scene and that staircase and who was there for that scene and who might have used the staircase before and after."

"There goes your alibi for all of us," said Gillian to Ronnie. "Somehow it always did seem too good to be true."

Chapter 11

THE MANAGER'S FLAT

The residential quarters of the manager of the Saracen's Head consisted of four rooms immediately above the entrance foyer and reception desk. They could be reached by a small staircase from the manager's office behind Reception or by a door from the maze of corridors and open areas on the first floor—a door that led directly into the sitting room. Des's murderer could have gained or been given access to the flat from either of these.

Superintendent Dundy had sent Nettles off to talk to the kitchen and the cleaning staff. Nettles was an excellent chap, but he did tend to chat, to comment, to make his presence felt. Dundy liked to sniff out a place in silence—walk around, get the feel, sense a personality. Then he would look around and think of what was missing, what was out of place. So he said to Charlie, down in Reception: "Let's go up and quietly get the lie of the land, shall we?" Charlie nodded, and together they ascended the stairs and went to work.

The manager's living quarters—or dying quarters, as

they had so soon become for Des Capper—had been in-
habited for twenty years by "dear old Arthur," as Gillian
Soames and others always called him, and his impress
was still on them. His had been the choice of furniture,
his the choice of the pictures on the walls. It was mainly
in the extras and inessentials that Des and Win had made
their tenure felt. Or that Des had made his tenure felt.

The photo of the hotel in Dubbo, squarely in the center of the sideboard, had Des standing by the wrought-
iron pillar of a wonderful nineteenth-century structure,
looking loathsomely proprietorial. Win was not to be
seen. Perhaps she was behind the camera, but as it
seemed a highly professional photograph—you could feel
the flies, smell the sheep-dip—this was unlikely. Probably
she had been behind the bar as usual. The books all
seemed to be Des's, too: *The Homemaker's Medical
Enquire Within, The Secrets of the Tarot,* Desmond
Morris, *Reader's Digest* evaporated books, L. Ron
Hubbard, and Arthur Hailey. Even the *Jane Fonda
Exercise Book* belonged, Dundy guessed, more to Des
than to Win. There were newish paperbacks of several
biographies of the Mountbattens, presumably purchased
to give corroborative detail to Des's recent incautious
claims, which Dundy had heard about from Frank. There
was also *Heat and Dust* and a popular book on Indian
religions.

Des's research for the festival took in heavier tomes.
From the Ketterick Public Library he had borrowed a
thick book on Donizetti by William Ashbrook and a volume on Elizabethan and Jacobean comedy. The latter had
been much renewed, with dates handwritten in. The for-
mer was a new borrowing, with a return date ten days
hence. They both sat on a small table by the biggest arm-

chair. Charlie took them up and skimmed through the sections on *Adelaide* and *The Chaste Apprentice.*

Iain Dundy was over by the sideboard, getting whiffs of Des's personality. There was a pile of old records there—Mantovani, James Last, and the Beach Boys—but the record player did not look as if it had been touched since they had moved in. The *Mirror* and the *Sun* of the day before were beside one of the easy chairs, and some old *Penthouses* were stacked under a coffee table. The racing pages of the newspapers were marked for possible bets. In one of the papers something was cut out; it seemed to be the regular medical column. Iain Dundy raised his eyebrows and went on.

Win's influence seemed mainly to consist of dainty linen and lace mats on the dressing tables, sideboards, and occasional tables, such as the one on which the knife had lain. Probably also hers were the antimacassars on the backs of easy chairs and sofa. Leaning against the sofa, Dundy found that the covering was slightly damp. The furniture in the room was all solid, capacious, and worn, and had no doubt served "dear old Arthur" for years, until it had now gained this light accretion of alien personality from the new managers. No doubt it was like this when a stately home was taken over by new stately owners.

The body had by now been taken away, though chalk marks and tapes marked where it had been, and Iain Dundy could remember it very well. The sitting room in the manager's flat was a large one, with the main bedroom leading off at one end, kitchen and second bedroom leading off from the other. The sofa and the easy chairs were clustered around a fireplace, with a small dining table and two chairs positioned by the window that overlooked Ketterick High Street. This left a goodly space at one end, where the stairs down to the ground floor and the door out to the corridor were. It was in this open space that Des's body had been found. It had pitched forward, its head towards the door into the corridor, its back decorated by a knife between the shoulder blades. The table on which had rested the knife had been in that open space too, just behind the sofa. One could still see the imprint left by the handle of the knife on the embroidered table mat it had rested on. Anyone, on an impulse born of overwhelming nausea or provocation, could have taken it up and stabbed the loathly Des with it on the spur of the moment.

Did the position of the body tell one anything? Could Des have been starting towards the door when he was stabbed from behind? Possibly. Equally, he could have been standing in thought, facing in that direction, and propelled sprawling forward by the force of the blow from behind. There was nothing particular to look at on that wall apart from the door and a reproduction of Morris's *Queen Guinevere* beside it. But a man in thought does not need anything to look at, and Des, Dundy suspected, was a man with a variety of projects demanding thought.

Did he, Dundy wondered, keep all these projects in his head, or did he keep some written record, however vestigial?

Dundy and Charlie spent over an hour circling the flat warily, like two animals careful not to invade the other's territory. Then Nettles came up after a not very rewarding session with the domestic staff and inevitably they all settled down to an interim comparing of notes. Dundy came out at once with the question of Des's projects and his thirst for scraps of knowledge.

"I don't think there can be any doubt," he said, "that he was a man who loved information. First of all, just information. Have you met people like that? Do they still exist in your generation? They'll bring it out anywhere, anytime: the age of the pyramids, the average number of eggs a chicken lays a year, the estimated population of China in the year 3000. Totally out of the blue they'll come out with it—some real conversation stopper. And like as not they'll just think they've floored you and congratulate themselves on their cleverness."

"I know that sort of bloke," agreed Nettles. "The sort who makes you slope off to the saloon bar if you hear his voice coming from the public. But in his case it shades off into something much more nasty, doesn't it?"

"Apparently. But I think it starts off as this sort of desire to accumulate out-of-the-way information. The sort of fact you got in the old Ripley "Believe It or Not" column or as a little paragraph in the *Reader's Digest*. That sort of interest is rather boring but totally innocent. When it spreads itself out and becomes a desire to collect information about living people, that's when it becomes dangerous. And so far as we can see, Des's magpie instincts about information also embraced people—the guests at the hotel and very probably the staff at the hotel as well."

"What I'm trying to get a handle on," said Charlie, "is the point of it all. I mean, with some people it can be just accumulation for the sake of accumulation. I wouldn't think it was that way with Des Capper, would you?"

"No," said Dundy emphatically.

"Then was it for pure, straightforward blackmail? Was it for chuckling over and poking ribs—as in Frank's story about the man who'd brought his bird here? Or was it something more subtle than either?"

"Yes, that is the question, isn't it? I suppose the murder gives us the answer to that, if we're on the right track." Iain Dundy paused and scratched his ear. "But perhaps it's not completely clear-cut, not as neat as you put it. You say: Did he accumulate grubby bits of information just for the sake of it, did he chuckle over it, or did he use it for blackmail? Perhaps the answer is: All three. It's not necessarily either/or. If the information was not usable, he just enjoyed having it. If it was usable, he had to decide what use to make of it."

"And there was one other possible use for it," said Charlie thoughtfully.

"What's that?"

"Revenge."

Dundy nodded.

"There is also this question of how he got appointed here," said Nettles. "It's something the staff keep bringing up. He wasn't just awful; he was the wrong type."

"We'll have to start looking at that," agreed Dundy. "If he was as unsuitable as Frank and everyone else imply, then the question of blackmail must surely arise there."

"And if it arises there, then the chances are that it has arisen again now," said Nettles.

"Yes, though let's remember one thing: That would be blackmail for personal advancement. It could be done very subtly. Just a whisper and a nod. It could be done so indirectly as hardly to be blackmail at all."

"Though not by this Capper character, surely, sir, if what we've heard of him is to be believed?" objected Charlie. "Hardly a subtle character, by all accounts."

"Probably you're right. But still, it is one further step to blackmail for money. A further and a very dangerous one. But if he was blackmailing one of the festival guests here, what else could it be but blackmail for money?"

Charlie coughed. "What the class newspapers call 'sexual favors,' sir?"

"Well, maybe," said Dundy. "I haven't had a very strong sexual whiff from this case yet. More a matter of sheer black bile, as far as Capper is concerned. But we'll have to talk to people and find out if that was one of his interests. I presume there are some reasonably attractive women around connected with the play in one way or another. His wife would be the last to know—or, on the other hand, she could be leading us on in a big way, don't forget. Still. I would like something just a little more definite than sexual favors."

"There's nothing written down, is there, sir?" asked Nettles. "No kind of record of the little things he found out?"

"That's what I've been wondering. Nothing's been handed over by the technical experts, and we haven't come across anything today. I wonder if he was the sort to write things down. What impression do you get?"

The other two frowned, then shook their heads. "No impression, sir," said Charlie regretfully. "Could have been a real little Samuel Pepys. Could have kept it all in his head."

"The sheer *amount* he seems to have accumulated might be a hopeful sign," said Nettles.

"Yes, and at least that generation's more likely to write things down than a younger one," said Dundy hopefully. "Youngsters these days need a keyboard connected to a screen if they want to remember anything. I suppose the first thing is to organize a search of all the obvious places—desks, drawers, sideboards, and so on. You take the big bedroom, Peace, you take the small one and the manager's office downstairs, Nettles, and I'll take this room and the kitchen. If we get no results, we'll start thinking of hiding places."

And so they got down to it. But of results in the obvious sense, there were none.

There were just a few things that they thought it worthwhile to collect up and mull over afterward. Des had apparently eaten All-Bran for breakfast and taken Ex-Lax regularly. He had used a mouth spray against bad breath, and an antiperspirant. His teeth were his own, but he used a toothpaste designed to remove heavy stains. There were many used packs of playing cards and a backgammon set. There were road maps with routes laboriously marked out, perhaps by Win. The routes, mostly from Carlisle, had not taken them to well-known beauty spots or places of tourist fame, not to Wordsworth's Cottage or Castle Howard. They had been exclusively to towns. When Dundy compared them to a leaflet downstairs on the reception desk, he found that they were all towns that boasted hotels in the Beaumont chain.

No harm in that, of course. Doubtless the Cappers would have got a reduction on their stays. But the fact that most of the routes were from Carlisle made Dundy wonder if they had been prospecting during Des's previous job, deciding which of the hotels they—or rather *he,* surely—was going to blackmail himself into the managership of.

On a personal level the only haul they got was a few letters and postcards. There was little any of them could make out of the postcards: one of the Alhambra with "Fantastic place—Kevin" on the back; one of Michelangelo's *David* with "Christ what a nancy boy, eh? Jacko." The postmarks were from the fifties, and they were addressed to hotels in Parkes and Coonabarabran, New South Wales. The only reason the policemen could see for keeping them had to be the pictures.

The letters were marginally more revealing. Three of them were from Des's mother. The latest, very feeble and practically without meaning, was addressed to Des and Win after their move to Britain in 1974. The earliest had also been addressed to Des in Britain—in fact, to a street in Pimlico. The date was December 1945, and it expressed the wish that he had waited until things were more settled before going "home":

> But then you always did what you want, but I hear such dreadful things on the wireless and wonder and with everything so short there are you getting enough to eat?

The other was addressed to Private Capper, of the Second Borderers, serving in India, apparently stationed near Bombay. So Des's army career had begun *after* the Second World War. Not the impression he had given Frank, the doorman. The letter expressed bewilderment as to why he had joined up:

> You always were a mystery to me, but one blessing youll be nearer home so when the three years are up you can come back, this is where you really belong son I hope youve learnt that by now with all love Your Ever Loving Mum.

The only other letter of interest was from India, dated 1947, and addressed to Corporal Capper, stationed in Hong Kong. After jocose preliminaries, it said:

You lucky bastard, getting out before it all turned nasty. My God, the things I've seen, but I expect you've heard from some of the boys, and you can believe it.

Don't write and tell me you're living the life of Riley in H.K., Des, because I don't want to know. You always were the kind of crafty bastard who could slip out from under.

Not this time, thought Dundy.

"Well," he said, shaking his head and looking at the meager haul "This is the sum total of finds of interest, and I can't say it gets us much further. No written notes of discoveries, no written evidence of any blackmail attempts. What does that mean? That he didn't write anything down?"

"Could be," said Nettles. "If he was a serious blackmailer, it would be much the wisest thing."

"Yes…" said Dundy. "Somehow the vibes I'm getting from this man don't suggest that he would always do the wisest thing…But maybe I'm getting him entirely wrong."

"I may be wrong, too, sir," said Charlie, "but the vibes I'm getting suggest that he was a very *obvious* man, for all his cunning. As I said before, not subtle at all. Awful in an obvious way…obvious minded, somehow."

"Sort of second-rate brain?" suggested Dundy.

"Yes, or third. You know, the sort of person who thinks it's true because he's read it in the papers. Quotes *Reader's Digest* as if it were the *Encyclopaedia Britannica.*"

"Oh, God, yes."

"That's how I see him. And I wonder—if he's taken notes of any sort, then it seems to me he's probably hidden them in a very obvious place. I mean the sort of places old ladies hide things, the places that are always the very first ones that the experienced burglar looks in."

"Kept under the geranium pot, do you mean?"

"Yes. Laughable, and a bit pathetic. Where in the house do old people hide their little bits of money, their pension books, their savings certificates?"

"The backs of cushions," said Nettles promptly. "Behind the books in the bookcase. Under the sofa cushions. Under the mattress. In the tea caddy. On top of the kitchen dresser."

"That's the sort of place. I just wondered, sir, whether it might be worthwhile looking there."

In the event, Charlie turned out to be right about the obviousness of Des's mind. Des and Win had gone in for Scandinavian-style beds, with the (hard) mattress laid straight onto a board. Good for the back, as Des would no doubt have told many a bar customer at length in his time. His notebook was pushed under the mattress, on top of the board. Apparently Win Capper had not had the aristocratic sensibilities of the princess who could not sleep on a pea. The notebook was on her side.

But there was no doubt it was Des's. Dundy took it downstairs and compared the handwriting with his entries in the hotel register. It was Des's hand, all right. Or fist, more likely. Because the little notebook, bound in green plastic, was mostly a jumble of jottings in no particular order and dubiously legible in places. These ill-spelled notes were *aides-mémoires* in the strictest sense. They seemed to be scribbled down pretty much anywhere, just as he felt the urge to commit things to memory. So that "Geary—gin?" came two or three pages after another note that read: "Geary—ten half bottles in six days *known.*" There was, then, no sequence or continuity, and Dundy and his two assistants had to get from it such isolated nuggets as they could. If they were baffled, it had to be said that Des was frequently, too. His bafflement expressed itself in such diagrams as:

$$\text{CARSTON G} \; - \; \text{CLARISSA}$$
$$/ \qquad\qquad \backslash$$
$$\text{SUSAN F.} \qquad\qquad \text{JASON T.}$$

Underneath the diagram there was scrawled the question "What gives???"

Question marks, in fact, were very frequent. There were "Gillian S.—Ronnie Wimsett??" There was "Fortnum—Natalya R.—phone calls—where?—expensive—what's up? Defecting?" Later, presumably connected with this, there was "Why Mallory not involved?" Mallory also appeared in "Mallory—Singh???" Underneath which was written: "Where?"

But there was one page in the book where there seemed to be some sort of organization, where the information seemed grouped around one central figure. There was a note that said: "Girls—young." Then he had added: "Constant supply—recruited by bodyguard. Bodyguard paid by the girls? Age?" This last word had been underlined many times. At the bottom of the page there was an enigmatic "HAD 9." What could that mean? That he'd had nine such assignations with classical music groupies to Des's knowledge? But there was a shaky arrow leading to the side of the page that suggested that this entry related to something on a previous page. In any case, it was overshadowed by an entry in red: Stretching from the bottom left hand corner to the top right, misspelled but sharp in impact, in letters that bit deep into the page as if they had been scrawled in a fury, there was the legend:

GET GOTLIEB

"I think we may have struck gold," said Iain Dundy.

Chapter 12

PEOPLE TALKING

For the actors it should have been a day of delicious anticlimax. It should have been a day for reading the early reviews, letting off a bit of steam, of shopping for unnecessaries. But it wasn't like that at all.

Reviews there were, luckily. Reviews that praised the "tireless energy" of the *Apprentice* cast, the "mature warmth and humanity" of Carston Galloway's Ralph Greatheart, and "the sense of a send-up of a parody" behind Ronnie Wimsett's chaste apprentice. The music critics had done their bit, too. There was acclaim for the "incredible and flamboyant richness" of Singh's voice and for the "golden opulence and vivid femininity" of Natalya in the letter scene. All these were lapped up, swapped, discussed, and disputed, though not by Clarissa Galloway, whose Melinda Purefoy was not mentioned at all.

But it was all, somehow, a bit academic. A bit of a sideshow. Because at half past eleven the superintendent, who had only been glimpsed hitherto walking purposively around the hotel, began interviewing people who he thought might be of help to him. And since the staff of the hotel had all been together at the crucial time and had been given a thorough going-over by one of his men, that left the actors and the residents. And of course, it was all quite ridiculous, but...but one really had to decide how much to tell him, didn't one? And one had to decide which of one's fellow actors one could talk to about how much to tell him. Probably it would be mostly routine, wouldn't it, and rather dreary, but then there would be those areas...

And it *was* mostly routine, this preliminary round of interviews. But there were areas in which Dundy and his men found tiny nuggets of interest.

"But I *can't* see," said Clarissa Galloway, "why we can't be interviewed together. We do everything together. Except sleep together, sometimes, but that goes in waves."

She crossed a shapely black-stockinged leg, doing it at Charlie Peace, as being the youngest man in the room. His eye gleamed with a spark of amused appreciation. Iain Dundy's mouth tightened. Of course with these arty people it all came back to sex in the end.

"I'm afraid interviewing you together would be quite against regulations," he said.

"It must be terrible to be so *bound* by regulations," said Clarissa with stage thoughtfulness.

"You say you do everything together, but in fact you weren't playing husband and wife in this play, were you?"

"Good God, no. Ralph Greatheart is an *ancient* character."

"Do your parts link up? Are you together onstage a great deal in the course of the evening?"

"No, we have a scene together at the end of the first act, but then we're hardly onstage at all together until the last act."

"Then were you offstage together a lot?"

"Oh, yes, a fair bit."

"Talking together in the dressing rooms behind the stage?"

"Well, I don't remember talking together," said Clarissa, again with that contrived thoughtfulness. "But of course terribly *aware* of each other. *Al*ways terribly aware. It's what distinguishes us as a partnership."

And that, Dundy suspected, was nothing but the truth, in spite of the stagy manner in which it was delivered.

"I see. While you were backstage, were you aware of anyone leaving the dressing room—the two dressing rooms, rather, in part of the kitchen and the private functions room—to go into the main part of the hotel?"

"No, I can assure you Carston didn't. As to the others—Well, of course there was young Peter Fortnum."

"Ah."

"*Quite* a talented beginning. Plays Peter Patterwit and has some quite *frightful* jokes, which is almost inevitable in this kind of comedy, but he carries them off rather well…"

"Yes, I'm sure. But it was his trip into the main part of the hotel you were going to tell me about."

"Was I?" She smiled dazzlingly at the three men. "Well, if you *want* to hear about it. It's surely of no importance. Let me see…He came offstage—it was towards Interval time, perhaps a quarter of an hour before—and

Connie Geary was complaining that she'd run out of gin. She's a dipso, poor old thing, though quite a happy one, which is a blessing when you see the other kind. Where was I? Oh, yes, Peter Fortnum had just come off, and he wasn't due to launch any more of his *leaden* innuendos at the audience until after the Interval, and he said straightaway that he'd go and fetch her a half which is what he did. Actually, it *did* seem to some of us that he was gone an awfully long time."

"I see," said Iain Dundy. "Well, no doubt it's something I shall be able to follow up. Now, about the dead man himself—what were your impressions?"

She leaned forward. She had decided that honesty would be the best policy and sincerity the best manner. She delivered herself of a great deal of sincerity.

"Quite frightful! A squirt, a pusher, a bore. And of course dreadfully inquisitive! I don't expect *that's* news to you, is it? He made no secret of it. Now, when you've been a *star* for...some years, as I have, as Carston and I have, you get used to inquisitiveness—from fans, from the press, and so on. But quite naturally some of the others here aren't *used* to it in the same way and react very badly to prying and snooping. I think you'll discover in the end that that's where the answer lies. His snooping was the death of him."

And a very satisfactory end, too, her dazzling smile to all three men seemed to imply.

"My movements?" said Brad Mallory. "My dear man, they are an open book and vouched for by thousands. I was in the Town Hall. I had a seat in the back row—in case I was needed behind the scenes. I had people beside me who would certainly remember me even though I didn't have any conversation with them. I should think Frank, the doorman, noticed me when I left, and I remember speaking to him when I returned at Interval."

"You actually left the concert at Interval?"

"Exhausted by the splendor of Singh's performance."

His hand flapped, like a vulture's wing.

"And you came straight back to the Saracen?"

"Yes."

"And then?"

"Straight to my room—to recover some degree of equilibrium."

Unvouched for by thousands, thought Dundy.

"Ralph Greatheart is, I suppose, the biggest part in the play," said Carston Galloway judiciously. He made it sound as if he were calculating the number of lines rather than being immodest. "I *think* it's bigger than the apprentice himself. So I'm onstage a great deal of the time. Last night, when I wasn't onstage, I was in the improvised dressing room backstage."

Iain Dundy was conscious of movement behind Galloway in the cramped quarters of the manager's room, which had been put at his disposal to conduct the interviews in. It was Charlie Peace, who had been making signs and who now cleared his throat.

"Yes, Constable?"

"If I may, sir, there's one question I would like to ask the gentleman. I should say that I happened to be in the audience last night. There is one time, isn't there, Mr.

Galloway, when you actually appear on the balcony? You and one or two others?"

"That's right. The upper stage. I included that, of course, when I talked of being onstage."

His manner was that of one rebuking an inattentive schoolboy. Nevertheless, he hadn't mentioned it, Dundy noted. If Peace hadn't been in the audience, would it have come up? He shot a grateful glance at Charlie, then took over the questioning again.

"This upper stage, sir—is it part of the regular balcony around the courtyard?"

"That's right. Divided off from the rest of the balcony by a couple of makeshift partitions."

"And reached through a bedroom?"

"That's right."

"And how, sir, did you reach that bedroom?"

"We went up a little service staircase in the corner of the kitchen. Apparently it's one that's used by the cleaning women and sometimes by the maids when they're taking up breakfasts in bed or room orders."

"I see. You say *we* went up, sir. Could you tell me who the other actors were who were on with you?"

"Oh, yes. It's a scene where the Greatheart family have been woken up at night by the horseplay of the apprentices, which of course has been taking place below on the main stage. It's a fairly traditional situation—"

"And your family in the play is—?"

"Joan Carley, who plays my wife—my stage wife— and Gillian Soames, who plays my daughter. Oh, and I think Jason Thark, the producer, followed us upstairs to see how the scene went."

The wonderful casualness of these arty people when they lob their grenades, Dundy thought!

"Ah, he would remain in the bedroom, I suppose?"

"Yes...Though now that you mention it..."

"Yes?"

"I seem to remember, as we all went into the bedroom, sounds from the corridor—almost like a row." He passed his hand over his forehead in one of those stage gestures that he and his wife specialized in, which set Dundy's teeth on edge. "No, it's too vague. Remember I was about to go out onto the balcony. It's a scene that calls for a lot, vocally and dramatically, so I was only thinking of that. You'll have to ask Jason."

And you've made quite sure that I do, thought Dundy.

"This Jason Thark is the man your wife says, er..."

"They've been sleeping together since we got here," said Carston indifferently.

"I see...And did you all go back to the kitchens together after the scene was over, sir?"

"Er, no. The ladies, you see, go twittering off quite early in the scene, after a drunken obscenity from Matthew Cotter, one of the apprentices—only it's an obscenity nobody understands any longer, so it rather misfires. After they go, I have several more minutes haranguing the lads; then I go in."

"And last night they'd already gone downstairs?"

"Yes."

"And then did you go down with Mr. Thark?"

"No...No, Jason must have gone down by that time. I went down to the kitchen alone."

"I see. About what time was this scene, Mr. Galloway?"

"Oh, good Lord, one doesn't notice times. Well on in the first half but not Interval by a long chalk. I may say that I spoke to little Soames the moment I got down to the bottom of the stairs. Asked her how she thought it'd gone."

"And you couldn't put a time to it, roughly?"

"Oh, say, five to eight, or eight—something like that."

"I see. Thank you."

Iain Dundy did not have to look down at his notes to remind himself of the police doctor's preliminary estimate of the time of death. He thought it had occurred at some time between eight and a quarter past nine.

❁ ❁ ❁

"I was in my bedroom," said Gunter Gottlieb. "I plan, I read the score, I *hear* the music to myself. So do I *feel* my way into the performance tomorrow—that is, tonight. Even Donizetti—which is piffle, pure piffle!— even Donizetti has to be *felt,* experienced, heard inside."

"I see," said the superintendent, feeling an intense dislike for the lean, arrogant figure sitting opposite him. "So you were here in the hotel, alone in your room, all evening?"

"Yes. Oh—one moment. A girl came."

"A girl? Her name?"

Gunter Gottlieb shrugged.

"I don't know."

'What did she come for?"

"Sex. We just have sex; then she go."

"I see. Was she a prostitute?"

"Certainly not. I don't use prostitutes."

"How did you meet this young lady, then?"

"Meet? I not meet her. I have sex with her. My body-guard, Mike, he got her for me."

"I see. He made all the arrangements?"

"Yes."

"When was this? How long did it take?"

"It was, oh, seven something. I suppose altogether it took about twenty minutes. It usually does."

"I see..." Iain Dundy sighed internally. He was being very honest, this repulsive man. Was a lack of hypocrisy to be commended in a matter like that? he wondered. "Tell me, Mr. Gottlieb, can you think of any reason why Mr. Capper should feel a particular dislike for you?"

"Who?"

"Des Capper, the dead man."

Again Gottlieb shrugged. "I have no idea."

"You did nothing to him?"

"I was quite unaware of his existence."

Dundy felt quick glances in his direction from both Nettles and Peace. That was a lie, surely. The hatred of that "Get Gottlieb" scrawl could only have come from some incident the man would be sure to remember. Did the lie spring from his prodigious arrogance? Or was it a clumsy attempt to disguise guilt?

"Oh, he was the most *horrible* little man," said Gillian Soames. She had decided that Iain Dundy was just the kind of man she liked and was talking a lot to cover the fact. "Well, not little at all—all too large. You know the type—the sort of man who, the moment he puts out his hand to shake yours, you know you don't want to touch. Shiversome. Yukky. But I'm talking nonsense. You must meet a lot more of that type than most of us."

Iain Dundy had relaxed considerably. This was the

sort of witness he liked: nervous, for some reason, but direct, reliable. Not arty at all, he told himself.

"Oh, I don't know," he said expansively. "Most of the people we meet are pretty average individuals. But it's interesting you should say that. When you connect him with the kind of people I meet, do you mean you thought there was something…criminal about him, right from the start?"

Gillian considered. "No, that would be going too far. I just took a dislike to him. Later on, when one heard of the man's snooping activities, one did start wondering what was the end in view."

"What snooping activities were these?"

"Oh, it was Clarissa who made the big fuss. He'd been snooping around in her room, she said, looking in drawers and so on. Occasion for big scene. But I'm sure on this occasion Clarissa was telling the truth. In fact, the more one took notice of him, the more he seemed to be snuffling around after information that might prove useful to him."

"May I test him on something?"

"Go ahead."

"He thought you might be having an affair with someone called Ronnie Wimsett."

Gillian laughed uproariously. Iain Dundy felt obscurely glad that Des Capper had been wrong, which was odd, because he had not yet swapped a word with Ronnie Wimsett. Behind Gillian's back a tiny glance passed from Charlie to Nettles and from Nettles back to Charlie. They recognized a sexual spark when they saw one. They were seeing one now.

"I take it he was wrong?"

"Of course. Want to know how he got the idea?"

"Yes."

"He was going round from table to table in the Shakespeare, pushing himself into all the conversations. That was my first evening here. When he got near our table, Ronnie and I held hands and looked into each other's eyes to keep him away. Somewhat surprisingly, it worked."

"Couldn't see below the appearances, eh?"

"Well, with the performance Ronnie and I put on, that's not surprising. I was just surprised he thought being in love was a sufficient reason for his staying away. But often he got things wrong even when nobody was trying to mislead him. Like when he oozed up to Peter Fortnum and me the day we arrived and assumed we must be 'the operatic lady and gentleman.' The fact that we were gazing reverently at the stage should have told him that we were actors. Still, it doesn't do to assume that everything he thought he'd found out was wrong."

Dundy sighed. "No. The likelihood is that in one case he hit the jackpot. And a lot of good it did him. Now, can we talk a bit about that scene in the play that takes place on the balcony?"

Gillian crinkled her forehead. "Yes, I assumed you'd want to talk about that. It's funny, you know, but we discussed and discussed how we—the actors—*couldn't* have done it, and yet we never thought of that scene or never admitted we realized its significance."

"It seems to me," said Dundy, "that you never thought of the staircase, either."

Gillian smiled at him self-deprecatingly. "You must think us very dim. But in fact there were a number of people sitting around the bottom of that staircase all the time, so it would have been pretty difficult to slip up it without being noticed. That scene, of course, was different; that was legitimate business."

"Can you tell me exactly what happened?"

"I'll try—as I remember it. I think we gathered at the foot of the staircase and all went up together. That was Carston, Joan, myself, and Jason following. I remember Carston being first into the bedroom and then being in there with him and Joan just before going out onto the balcony..."

She became silent.

"You don't remember Mr. Thark being there?"

"No. I have to be honest, don't I? I remember, just before we went on, hearing voices in the corridor. Angry voices."

"And the other voice?"

'Well, it *could* have been Des Capper."

"You can't be more definite than that?"

"No, it wouldn't be fair to."

"And when the scene was over?"

"Joan and I came out first. Joan went down, and I watched a minute or two more of the scene through the window. Then I went down, too."

"Do you remember when Mr. Thark and Mr. Galloway came down?"

"No. I went to talk to Connie Geary. Jason may even have been back in the kitchen already. But I'm afraid I didn't notice at all."

Charlie Peace cleared his throat. "Mr. Galloway remembers coming up to you after he came down, miss. To ask you how you thought it had gone."

Gillian frowned. "Oh, yes. I think you're right. He did come up at some stage. I'm sorry I can't remember exactly when."

"You're a good, careful witness," said Dundy.
Or a clever one, thought Charlie.

"I sang," said Singh.

He looked towards the mirror at the far end of the manager's office and was annoyed to find it angled to reveal whether there was anyone standing at Reception outside. So it was reserved for Iain Dundy to gaze on that smooth light brown skin, those doelike dark eyes, those perfect girlish features, that plump, underexercised body. Singh brought back all his distrust of "arty" people that Gillian Soames had done so much to banish.

"Yes, I realize you sang," he said, his irritation showing through for the first time that day, perhaps because subconsciously he was judging Singh to be as yet a person of little importance in any world. "I gather your arias were towards the end of the first half, is that right?"

"*At* the end. So the applause could go on."

"I see. So that would mean you were singing from just before eight, maybe, till about—what?—ten past?"

Singh shrugged. "Probably."

"What were you doing for the rest of the time?"

"I was sitting in the room for the artists. All the time. They were asking me about my voice, my technique. It is very extraordinary. And at Interval there were impresarios and theater directors talking about possible offers of engagements. I was never alone."

He smiled a catlike smile. The pleasure seemed not in having an alibi but in being so sought after. If what he said was true, and it seemed likely, Dundy thought he would not need to interest himself very much in Singh. It would in any case be impossible to be as interested in him as he was himself.

"Darling, it would be totally irresponsible of me to say *any*thing," said Connie Geary. She smiled at him with the art of one who had once cared if she pleased men. "I am a totally reliable actress: I get on and off the stage when I should, and I never slur my lines. But apart from that I live in a *haze.* If you ask me 'Was he or she around at such and such a time?' I can only give you an impression. *If that.*"

"I see." Dundy sighed.

"And that wouldn't be fair."

"No. It's a pity, because you were around in the kitchen most of the time."

"Yes, I was. I only have three scenes, though *very* meaty ones. But I can't tell you anything definite about what went on backstage because it wouldn't be right."

"Do you remember sending Mr. Fortnum for more gin?"

"Oh, yes, though I don't remember when."

"Do you remember whether he took a long time?"

"Darling, it *seemed* an age!"

"Sure I took a long time," said Peter Fortnum.

He was firm spoken and fresh faced, and all Iain Dundy's experience told him he was about to tell lies. The same half look that had passed between him and his men when Gunter Gottlieb was talking now passed again.

"Why should it take so long? The maids say you ran through the kitchens and dining room."

"Superintendent, would you like to try an experiment? Send one of your policemen here to find room 146 and see how long he takes."

Dundy smiled. "I may do that. But it wouldn't be quite the same thing, would it? My men have probably never been in the residential part of the hotel. You have been here nearly a fortnight."

"It doesn't help," protested Peter. "You never get used to it. You think you've got it taped, and then it throws down a nifty one and you're lost again. And anyway, my room is on the second floor, and Connie's is on the first. I just got lost looking for it."

"Miss Geary's room is, as you say, on the first floor. It is also not that far from the door into Des Capper's flat. Did you go anywhere near that door?"

"No."

"How can you be so sure if you were lost?"

An expression of irritation crossed Peter's face. "Not knowingly, I mean."

"Did you see anyone while you were searching for room 146?"

Slight but perceptible pause.

"No."

"Well, well." Iain Dundy shifted in his chair. There were lies being told here, but for the moment they were not nailable lies. "Let's get on to something else. I believe you've been helping a bit as translator for the Russian lady."

Another tiny pause.

"That's right."

"Including at rehearsals for the opera—whatever it's called?"

"Adelaide di Birckenhead." Peter pronounced the name with relish. "Yes, I went along there when I could."

"Tell me, can you give me any reason why Des Capper should feel particularly bitter about Herr Gottlieb?"

Peter settled back more easily in his chair. "Oh, yes. Yes, I can. It was just a few days ago, actually. I was in the wings, and there had been one of Gottlieb's scenes. You've talked to Gottlieb?" Dundy nodded. "Then you can probably guess what they're like. Icy, premeditated murder. I don't think Des Capper saw the scene; otherwise he might have been more careful. Most of the cast were onstage, and Mallory and Singh had gone up, too. Capper came up behind me, saw Singh onstage, and made some remark about not realizing there were Indians in medieval Birckenhead. 'Running the corner shops, I suppose.'" Peter's imitation, like Gillian's earlier, brought the dreadful Des momentarily but vividly to life. "Typical barroom joke, and just the sort of thing that Des would think was clever."

"Just one moment. What was Capper doing backstage?"

"Exercising his right as a member of the festival committee to go anywhere and watch anything. I gather this is a right nobody else exercises. Anyway, eventually there was a break—God, we needed it!—and when I got to the Green Room, there was Des already there, irritating the hell out of everyone, particularly the poor American tenor who had been the main victim of Gottlieb's scene. That's when it happened."

"The incident."

"Yes, the row. Gottlieb was having a discussion—No, Gottlieb was *telling* the director of the festival that he intended changing the opera scheduled for the next festival to *Fidelio.* It was typical Gottlieb unreasonableness. The director was beginning to get a bit heated when Des stepped forward. Trying to mediate, so he said."

"Ah, and Gottlieb—?"

"Bawled him out. Sheer barrack-room stuff. Get out, don't come near my rehearsals again, that kind of thing. If it had been anyone else, there'd have been applause."

"And how did Des Capper take it?"

"With Gottlieb you don't have much choice. He slunk out."

"Meditating revenge, do you think?"

"I know so. He practically said so later, said he'd learned all he needed to know about revenge in India in 1947. Des tended to go on about India."

Iain Dundy sat considering. Then he threw a bouncer. "Tell me, sir, why have you been making so many expensive phone calls since you came here?"

Peter Fortnum blinked at the change of subject but had his answer—Dundy could have sworn to it—prepared.

"My girlfriend is in Germany. She is with a theater company in Stuttgart."

"She must have very good German."

"She is advising on costumes. For a production of *The Merry Wives of Windsor.*"

"It's remarkable that you can afford all these calls. You're a young actor, and I believe you have quite a small role."

"Is it so remarkable?" Peter asked. "With a name like Fortnum?"

Superintendent Dundy reminded himself that from one point of view all an actor's performing life is living a lie.

"You're damned right I wasn't going to tell you," said Jason Thark. "And don't, for God's sake, ask why not, because it's bloody obvious, isn't it?"

"Well, let's get the facts clear first, shall we, sir? You went upstairs with the three actors who were about to appear in the balcony scene."

"That's right."

"But you never followed them into the bedroom?"

"No, because I saw Des Capper coming along the corridor. There was something about him—something pushy and self-satisfied—and so I lingered by the door. I'd heard about a set-to between him and Gottlieb at the Alhambra. He had the cheek to say, 'After you,' and make to go into the bedroom as well."

"Which in a way you might say he had a right to do," said Iain Dundy in fairness to the dead Des.

"In a way. With any other manager I might have admitted the right: it was his place, as the Alhambra wasn't. But give Capper an inch and he took a mile. He'd been barging in everywhere pretending he had a right as a member of the festival committee. Next thing would be he'd demand to sit onstage, as the noblemen used to. So I gave him the rounds of the kitchen and told him to stick to his quarters."

"How did he react to that?"

"How do you think? He bridled, muttered, threatened, but in the end he trotted off."

"And you, sir? What did you do?"

"I was rather pleased with the whole affair, quite frankly. It made a good addition to the 'grand remonstrance' that the cast and I were going to address to the festival committee when the festival was over."

"Grand what, sir?"

"A sort of general complaint by the actors and the other people staying here. A letter to the powers that be in the Beaumont hotel chain and to the festival committee as well. So I went away to one of those little alcoves the place abounds in, one where there was a writing desk, and wrote down the threats that Capper had made and the ridiculous rights he claimed."

"I see, sir. Do you still have this memorandum?"

"Yes, as a matter of fact I've got it on me."

As he took it, Dundy was under no illusions. The memorandum could have been written ten minutes ago.

"Any thoughts?" Dundy asked his men when at last they were alone.

They looked at each other.

"On the face of it, Mallory seems the best bet," said Charlie Peace slowly. "Alone in his hotel room from around eight-fifteen till Interval time and after. If we take it Capper was killed by Interval, that gives him a quarter of an hour to do it in."

"Oh, and by the way, he poked his head in at the Shakespeare Bar on the way up," said Nettles. "Dawn told me that. Perhaps he wasn't just *exhausted* by Singh's performance, after all."

"Looking for someone?"

"Dawn couldn't say, of course. He said nothing. But maybe he was looking for Des."

"And maybe he found him," said Dundy.

"I'm not sure, on thinking about it, why I picked on Mallory as the best bet," said Charlie. "After all, there are at least three others who had good opportunities to get at Des as well. Carston Galloway after the balcony scene—and *didn't* the Galloways chuck around innuendos about the other actors? Then there's Fortnum, of course, when he went to get the gin. And Gunter Gottlieb any time after his girl left. He, in a way, had the most opportunity and was the least accounted for."

"Yes, but can you see anyone arranging an assignation like his was just before committing a murder? If, of course, he did intend committing it. The trouble is, we know of no reason for Gottlieb to kill Capper. He'd seen him off. It would make more sense the other way round: Gottlieb as victim."

"A highly popular corpse," commented Nettles.

"One thing, though," said Charlie thoughtfully. "If the key to all this is in Des's determination to 'Get Gottlieb,' then it may be we're paying too much attention to the play and not enough to the opera. Perhaps we should forget the actors for a bit and take a look at the singers."

Chapter 13

THE DIRECTOR'S OFFICE

"**A**nyone for the opera?" asked Dundy.

Evening had come, and weariness set in.

"Er, my wife has just had a baby," said Nettles.

"Of course. I'd forgotten."

"It is the fourth, but I'd quite like to see it."

"Oh, Lord. Haven't you seen it yet?"

"Only got the message as I was coming in this morning." Nettles shrugged. "Policeman's lot. Policeman's wife's lot."

"What about you, Peace?"

"Try anything once. But we're not going to get seats, are we?"

"We'll try to get them to slot us in somehow."

Dundy had begun to feel that the line of interviewees would stretch out to the crack of doom. It was all too much. There were others to interview, but they could wait: One of them needed a Russian interpreter. Ronnie Wimsett seemed to have been onstage much of the evening, and never on the upper stage. Gunter Gottlieb's heavy would at least have made a change after all the arty people, a reversion to familiar territory after uncharted shores. But he couldn't see that Gunter's girl was of much significance. She had apparently come and gone well before the earliest time the murder could have been committed. And it hadn't been anything more than a quick dip, for either of them, so far as he could see.

Sitting for a moment in the little manager's office, Nettles having scurried off, Charlie standing waiting for some action, Dundy meditated on the unattractive figure of the world's next "great conductor." He realized that all such figures had two sides, the artist and the private man, and that with Gottlieb the private man trailed badly last. He wondered briefly at such an unadulterated swine being the mediator between great composers and the ordinary man. He seemed to remember that a lot of musicians had behaved very badly in Nazi Germany. Then he shook himself and put aside the thoughts as unprofitable.

"I'll ring the festival office," he said. "See if something can be arranged."

"Well, of course," said the voice on the other end of the line, "the director of the festival is very busy, because it is the first night of the opera. That's what he's doing at the moment. He's down at the Alhambra seeing that the critics get their creature comforts and welcoming distinguished guests: Lord Harewood is coming, and Lord Goodman, and all sorts of people like that. On the other hand, I do know that he's very concerned about this murder, concerned that it shouldn't cast a cloud over the festival…"

"Ha!" said Dundy to Charlie as they collected together their notebooks and got ready to leave the Saracen for the first time that day. "Cast a cloud over the festival! Murder never casts a cloud over anything! As far as the mob coming here is concerned, it'll be a great bonus. Murder is the great British spectator sport, the ultimate in good clean fun."

Walking past the copper on the door and out into the pale evening sunlight, they found they had to cope with cameras and media persons stationed outside. One reporter looked pointedly and hopefully at their wrists ("Black held in Aussie slaying"), while another pursued them along High Street with questions. "Wrong man, sorry," lied Dundy, and they managed the rest of the five-minute walk in peace.

By now it was nearly seven o'clock, and the audience was flocking around and into the blue-and-maroon little theater, splendid, yet slightly dotty. Charlie looked at the audience curiously. It was certainly not like the Covent Garden audience—not dressy and ignorant. Charlie had got the measure of a Covent Garden audience in his younger days, when he had done duty for a ticket tout in Floral Street on a Pavarotti night. This audience was very different. There was the odd sprinkling of black-tie-and-long-skirt couples, but in general this was a young people's festival and a mecca for enthusiasts and cranks. Dress was casual, even colorful. Dundy, too, watched them for a moment; then they both slipped through into the foyer. Here Dundy gave a discreet message to one of the attendants, to be passed on to the director. Then they made for a deserted corner to wait for the rush to subside.

"My mother used to play Bingo in a place like this," said Charlie cheerfully. "This one's gone uphill."

The director Dundy could point out to Charlie, having seen his picture in the *Ketterick Evening Post.* He was a comfortable, candid-looking man, with just a hint of being worried out of his life, which Iain Dundy could quite understand, granted what much of his life must be like. He was standing by the stairs welcoming faces in the audience that he recognized. There were many of these, for the festival thrived on its regulars, and they seemed as pleased to see him as he apparently was to see them. The audience was as comfortable-looking as the director. They were mostly discussing the singers and waxing lyrical about the particular canary they fancied.

"It's a bit like a sports meeting," said Charlie. "People comparing Cram with Coe."

"And going all the way back to Bannister," agreed Dundy. "Some of these people sound like canary fanciers from way back, or gramophone freaks who collect seventy-eights. It wasn't like this in the old days. They've built up these audiences, just as the Saracen has."

For Dundy had been to the festival opera years before, when he had had a wife to buy tickets and the tickets had miraculously coincided with an evening off. The opera had been Donizetti then, too—*Don Sébastien, Roi de Portugal* ("like listening to a mouse trying to roar"—*The Observer)*. Dundy had rather enjoyed it, but he remembered the audience's commentary as being more bemused than informed.

Eventually the forward-moving stream thinned, the director's genial greetings became fewer, and the noise of the orchestra's tuning up penetrated through the doors into the auditorium. Last-minute arrivals, scuttling through, managed no more than a smile and a nod at the director. He looked towards Dundy, raised his eyebrows, then nodded up the stairs. Dundy and Charlie went over, and all three went on thick red pile up to the circle, then through a door that led them into a maze of corridors out of bounds to the general public. Eventually they came to a door labeled "Festival Director," and Charlie and Dundy were ushered into a tiny but cozy office with a desk piled with reference books and telephone directories and with room in front of the desk for only a couple of chairs. The walls were decorated, like London Italian restaurants, with publicity photographs of opera singers.

"I have a little office at the Saracen as well," explained the director, making them comfortable and pouring them both neat whiskeys from a bottle in the filing cabinet. "But somehow it's been less pleasant working there since poor old Arthur died."

Dundy was willing to hear just one more verdict on the unlovable Des.

"The new manager?" he asked. "Our popular corpse?"

"Exactly. I'm sure you've got the general idea by now. An appalling know-all, a peddler of folk wisdom and quack remedies, a one-man popular informer."

"And a great collector of inconvenient information about people," added Dundy.

"Yes, I—" The director hesitated, looked at Dundy, and then plunged in. "I suppose you remember the case earlier this year when my daughter was accused of shoplifting?"

"Yes, I was sorry you got all that publicity. I wasn't involved."

"Of course not. I don't blame the police. But she'd just lost a baby, had postnatal depression—Anyway, it made a good story for the local papers, and damn the consequences for her. It was all perfectly public, but what made it worse was Des coming up at the first committee meeting after the magistrates' hearing. 'Terribly sorry to hear about your little family trouble. As a father myself I can sympathize.' All done in a nicely raised voice. I could have—Well, no, I couldn't. But I *felt* like it then."

"I had no idea Capper had children."

"Nor had anyone. Maybe it was just a fiction to justify the sympathy. If he has, he seems conveniently to have cast them off, or it off, somewhere along the line."

Dundy looked at Charlie. He knew that both of them were toying with the entrancing notion of Des having fathered Singh during his time in India. Dundy shook his head and put the notion from him. Singh was about twenty years too young.

"You have no idea how he came to be appointed?" he asked.

"None. It's something all of us on the committee have discussed, I can tell you. We could only assume some hold on the chairman or managing director of the Beaumont chain."

"Blackmail, you mean?"

The director looked mildly horrified, as if such a thought had at least not been put into words hitherto.

"Oh, come, come," he said. "It didn't have to be anything so dramatic. He could have done somebody some service."

"Saved his son and heir from drowning?" said Dundy cynically.

"That sort of thing. Saved his life in the disturbances at the time of Indian independence. He waxed very eloquent about his experiences at Mountbatten's right hand."

"Hmmm," said Dundy. "Very *Jewel in the Crown*. As

a matter of fact, I wouldn't mind betting Capper got his notions of what happened at independence time from that TV series. He wasn't in India at the time; he'd gone on to Hong Kong. You mentioned his characteristic as almighty know-all and crushing bore. But it wasn't those in particular that annoyed the festival committee, was it?"

"No, though it was embarrassing, because he was pig ignorant, and we had to find ways of listening to him pontificating about things he knew bugger-all about. No, it was his pushiness and his prying that touched us on the raw. He took it as his right to go everywhere, poke his nose in everything."

"Did he have such a right?"

The director shrugged. "In theory, maybe. No other member of the committee would have *thought* of exercising it. But Des went everywhere, got to know everything, and *gave his advice.*"

Dundy waved his hand in the direction of the auditorium, whence pale echoes of vocal glory penetrated even to the director's office.

"I gather on occasion he poked his nose into rehearsals of the opera we can hear now."

"Oh, yes. I don't know how often. I was down here one day watching rehearsals and waiting to see that swine Gottlieb afterwards. There was a nasty moment, with Gottlieb humiliating the tenor, who had to be brought to the front of the stage if he was to be heard, and Mallory having to placate the soprano. The producer was rearranging positions, and suddenly I saw Des was there in the wings. I remember my heart sinking and thinking: Des is all we need at this stage."

"We've heard about this little episode," said Dundy.

"And about what happened afterwards in the Green Room."

"Do you remember exactly what Gottlieb said to Capper?" asked Charlie.

"Pretty well. 'I do not take advice from taverners'—I remember that. 'You come near one of my rehearsals ever again and I have you…thrown out on your fat bottom.' He has the men who could have done it, too."

"Did Capper say anything?"

"Nothing to the purpose. 'Sorry, I'm sure,' or 'No offense'—something like that. He just slunk away."

"But hoping to get his revenge," said Dundy. "We've evidence of that. He didn't like public humiliation."

"Who does? But with Capper it would have been a strong emotion, I'm sure. He nursed grudges."

"Yes." Dundy looked at him straight. "Tell me, if you were out to 'get' Gunter Gottlieb—"

"As, God help me, I may be yet."

"—how would you do it?"

The festival director considered. "I think my first reaction would be to say: hit him professionally."

"Ah! That's what I wondered. Because he is, shall we say, vulnerable, on his personal side, too, isn't he?"

"Girlies," said the director, shaking his head. "I know. It's something I've had to be very aware of. It's the popular press I fear: Royals and vicars and people in the arts world—those are the ones the tabloids have a particular down on. He seems impregnable, but that could be his Achilles heel. That's why I had a word about it with his minder—"

"Ah! You did that?"

"It seemed the sensible thing. I discovered that he was thick as two planks, but he had learned enough about

the law to know how to keep on the right side of it when
he had a mind. So I made it clear to him: nobody under-
age. And preferably nobody local. I think he's been
recruiting from the groupies who followed him from
Coventry and from people here for the festival. Gottlieb's
needs are occasional and brief."

"So that's made him pretty near impregnable on the
personal side, you think? That's why you'd go for him on
the professional side if you had to?"

"Yes, because odd though it may seem, the festival is
important to him. It's part of his overall strategy, and he
wants to be a success here, make it *his* festival."

"How did you come to appoint him?"

"That's easily explained. It seemed such a coup! He
came with the Midlands Orchestra last year and gave a
quite wonderful concert. Mahler and Beethoven—the
most thrilling Seventh you can imagine. Our regulars
were over the moon: It was the sort of glorious music-
making they heard in their dreams, one of them said. Our
regular opera conductor was off to be resident chief of
one of the state orchestras in Australia, so there was a
vacancy to be filled. Not expecting him to accept, we
approached Gunter Gottlieb."

"And he accepted?"

"Not immediately. He thought for three days, then
accepted provided he had charge of all the musical side of
the festival. That seemed like a wonderful bonus to all the
committee. We couldn't believe our luck."

"I take it you've learned better since?"

The director thought a bit, trying to be fair. "It would
be wrong to say that. I think this festival will probably be
a great success from a musical point of view. The opera
will, too: He makes Donizetti sound as good as mature

Verdi. But it will all be a personal success for himself, and to some extent it will be manufactured."

"You mean he brings his own fans, and so on?"

"Well, yes, he does, but I didn't mean that. There are four orchestral concerts, and the third will be given by the Welsh Symphony Orchestra. At the planning stage he insisted that they give *Death and Transfiguration* and insisted, too, that we engage Ernest Petheridge to conduct. Between ourselves, never the brightest conductor, and now, at seventy-five...Well, he can be relied on to endow the idea of eternity with new degrees of tedium. They'll be snoring in the aisles. *Then,* two nights later, the final concert, with Gunter Gottlieb conducting *Also Sprach Zarathustra*—surefire popular success, brilliant orchestral showpiece, and of course brilliantly conducted. And don't get me wrong—it will be. But it will *seem* that bit more brilliant by comparison. You get me?"

"Oh, I get you."

"And then, of course, there's the business of next year."

"That was what the row was about in the Green Room, wasn't it?"

"Disagreement...Well, yes, row. Except that I did manage not to lose my cool. It would mean changing the whole direction and character of the festival. You probably know what sort of festival Ketterick has had up to now: a festival for families and enthusiasts, with something for everyone. Some of the sillier critics sneer at the operas we do, but they're wonderfully direct and involving—first-rate theater. Gottlieb's is an attempt to change all that and put us in the international league. And, of course, it put us in a cleft stick."

"How?"

"If we say no and lose him, all the arts establishment and all the newspaper people will say we've opted for safeness and provinciality and second-rateness. If we say yes, we hand the festival to him on a plate, the rest of us become ciphers, and we betray our existing audiences."

"Yes, I see. An impossible decision. And I take it an impossible gentleman to work with?"

"Bloody impossible, between you and me. I think we'd be justified in turning him down and letting him go if only because he's obviously using us as a stepping-stone to something else and because it will certainly all end in tears, and pretty soon, too."

"So your view is that he's totally geared to being a success in his professional life and if you hit him there you would really touch him where it hurts? Something along those lines was my conclusion, too. He's a man programmed to succeed. He's to be the next—who's the bee's knees?—Karajan?"

"The comparison has occurred to other people. At the moment, his whole being is intent on two glorious successes: first the opera, then the final concert, where he'll hope to have people standing and cheering, led by his own groupies. Which he almost certainly will. And to be fair to him, which isn't easy, almost all of it will be deserved."

"He is good?"

"He is *very* good. He rides roughshod over everyone, but he is almost always right. And yet there is still…somehow—I can't put it simply—a lack. An emptiness…And I wonder whether in the long run music lovers aren't going to find this out…Would you like to see him doing a bit of the opera?"

"There can't be any seats, surely?"

"There's mine. I have to go and see to the Interval jamboree for nobs and critics. You've no idea how we butter up the critics from the big newspapers. You can have my seat until the break." He turned to Charlie. "And you can stand at the back, if you don't mind that. It's not usually allowed, but we can explain to the fire people that you're a policeman."

"I'm used to standing about," said Charlie. "I was in uniformed branch for a year."

"I think we'll say yes," said Dundy. "Though I'm not sure that I'm musical enough to understand this...this lack that you talk of."

They went back to the front of house, down the staircase, and along the corridor that spanned the back of the stalls. The director collected programs for Dundy and Charlie and then, with practiced stealth, opened the door into the stalls. As the music washed over them, he pointed Charlie to a place by the door and then led Dundy down to an aisle seat three rows down. Then he himself evaporated to attend to the wants of the important visitors.

Once settled, Dundy found himself cocooned in a devout attentiveness. This audience was a totally committed one. Onstage, and close to the front of the stage, a very personable tenor was emoting in slow time, sighing his way towards a close. Iain Dundy had only a smattering of holiday Italian, but he had an awful feeling that the tenor was boasting about how much his love had cost him. The cad, he thought. Then the orchestra hotted things up, and an attendant or junior terrorist rushed onstage to deliver an urgent message, of which the words *Inglese* and *Birckenhead* could be distinguished. At which the tenor leapt to his feet and with a skirl of his (unhistorical) kilt began delivering a martial cabaletta that taxed his sweet voice to the uttermost. When it was over, there was polite applause, the curtain came down, and dimmed lights came up while changes were made to the permanent set.

In the half-light at the back of the theater Charlie read the program. He had got a rough idea of the story from the volume in Des's sitting room: The personable hero, he remembered, would be Robert the Bruce, on the run from the English and about to take refuge, disguised, at *il castello di Birckenhead* the power base of his rival, who was also the husband of the woman he loved. Well, that was all clear, wasn't it? He turned to the history of the opera and immediately found himself gripped in a way he did not quite understand. He read through the account of the first version of the opera, then the story of the recent rediscovery of the later version. Only when he had finished that did he begin to realize that the break had been rather long. Looking up from his program, he found he was not alone in this feeling. In the Victorian intimacy of the Alhambra Theatre everyone could see everything, and even from the back of the stalls Charlie could see the figure of Gunter Gottlieb, his baton steadily beating on the open pages of his score in patent irritation. No doubt Gottlieb had decreed no more than two minutes for the break, and it had stretched out to four. But then the lights went down, there was a perceptible relaxation of tension in the audience, and Gottlieb raised his baton for the last scene before Interval.

In the previous scene, Charlie, for all his lack of knowledge of opera, had been conscious of a shimmering beauty that Gottlieb extracted from the very simple accompaniment to the tenor aria. Now he began to notice something very different. The curtain had risen on the peasants and retainers of the castle of Birckenhead (all kilted—in defiance not only of historical but also of geographical probability). They were celebrating something or other, probably Hogmanay, in song and dance. The stage picture was supposed to be one of uninhibited revelry, but what Charlie was most conscious of was the *lack* of real spontaneity. What impressed him most was the drilled nature of the performance—the military precision of the drumbeats, the terrified accuracy of the chorus, which at times affected their acting. It was as if—another historical absurdity—the opera was being performed by the soldiers of Frederick the Great for their commander in chief. One might see Gottlieb as the Prussian bandmaster writ large. Charlie did not quite see things in those terms, but he did register to himself: Everyone is bloody terrified.

He stood there, drinking it in, thinking that he might be able to make a habit of this kind of music if he ever got the opportunity. There was a scene for a dreadful comic servant, and then the baritone and soprano arrived to join the merrymaking, exuding manorial graciousness. The baritone found time to snarl something about *"gl'Inglesi"* to a retainer out of the corner of his mouth, in the way baritones have. Then suddenly the sound of merrymaking died away. The tenor had arrived. He stood for some moments at the back of the stage, commented on by everyone in hushed tones. Then he advanced to the front in what Charlie recognized as a clumsy but necessary maneuver. Soon he was launching into the great, swaying tune:

> *Io son pari ad uom cui scende*
> *Già la scure sulla testa.*

This was the moment, Charlie felt sure, that Des had come in on in rehearsal. Standing there in the darkness, letting the music lap over him and swaying in time to its irresistible impulse, Charlie thought that he might have had the glimmerings of an idea.

Chapter 14

THE CORRIDORS

"'The trivial round, the common task, should furnish all we ought to ask,'" misquoted Dundy under his breath next morning. And in future it bloody well will. Here we go on another load of backstage chitchat, shortly homing in on more accounts of what gives with the Galloways. At least when I rowed with my wife it tore us apart, because we meant it. With these arty people, who knows when they mean *anything?*

And what gives with Peace this morning? His mind isn't on it. And this girl's a perfectly personable little thing...He dragged his mind back to the interview he was conducting.

"As far as the balcony scene is concerned, I inspected them all before they went up the stairs," Susan Fanshaw was saying. "They were all in night gear, so it was quite straightforward. Then I was off hither and yon doing other things. The apprentices were onstage—onstage and off, because it's a very busy scene, and I have to see whether the costumes have suffered in the horseplay, whether they've lost anything, and so on. So though normally I might have noticed when Carston at least came back down the stairs, that night I didn't."

Iain Dundy coughed a dry, diplomatic cough.

"Er, you say normally you might have noticed?"

Susan obviously wanted to get that part of the discussion over with.

"Oh, Carston and I are vaguely sleeping together."

"I see. I had, actually, some idea of this, but perhaps you could put me into the picture. I gather his wife knows?"

"Oh, yes. Everybody knows. It's no great passionate affair. I mean, Carston is nice—" She pulled herself up. "No, not nice exactly, because he's mean as hell, and vain as well. Still, he *is* a wonderful actor, when he's fully stretched, whereas she will never in essence be more than a rep queen, for all her name. So it *is* rather exciting; it is decidedly a pleasant interlude…Not least because of his vast experience."

"Ah…You don't mean acting? No. Er, you don't mind being one of a long line?"

"Not at all. It's part of the thrill."

Iain Dundy sighed. He was never going to understand these people, still less like them. His bewilderment was increased when Susan Fanshaw added: "A long, long roster. Both male and female."

He drew his hand along his forehead. "I see. Then Galloway is—?"

"Predominantly hetero, but he takes it as it comes. He covers the waterfront, like Brad Mallory. It's pretty common in the theater."

"Oh, then Mr. Mallory—?"

"Must be the same. He doesn't make much secret of being besotted with young Singh—not even from you, I imagine. But I know an actress who had a pretty serious affair with him five or six years ago." She saw Dundy's face and laughed. "It must make it pretty difficult for you."

"All in a day's work," said Dundy bravely. "So you are sleeping with Mr. Galloway, and I gather Mrs. Galloway is sleeping with the producer, and this is all out in the open and talked about quite unashamedly?"

"Yes. What a lovely word: 'unashamedly'! So you think we should be ashamed? Of course, Clarissa uses the situation to launch lethal little barbs against Carston and me, but that's just her nature."

"I find it difficult," said Dundy, trying not to sound prim, "to get a picture of this marriage. Why do they stay together if they're quarreling all the time?"

"Haven't you ever met a soldier who's only happy in action? Or a policeman who couldn't be happy on the beat in a quiet area but is always itching for a bit of action?"

"Frequently."

"Well, then. 'Pleased with the danger when the waves went high / He sought the storms; but for a calm unfit...' Dryden. It's quite impossible to imagine either of the Galloways having a *calm* relationship with anyone."

"I see," said Dundy, sighing. "My point in trying to establish how open all this is, is to make the point that there was very little mileage to be got—by Des Capper, for example—out of threatening to reveal the truth of the situation to any of the people involved."

"None whatsoever. We all knew. The whole hotel, down to the kitchen skivvies, knew. The room maids probably had a running bet on as to who would be sleeping with who each night."

"Right…Right…So if any of you had a grudge against Capper, it would have to be on some other grounds."

"Oh, certainly. Like that he was the biggest bore, the biggest ignoramus, and the biggest liar in a fifty-mile radius."

"I doubt whether people get murdered for any of those reasons," said Iain Dundy. "And I suppose if there were anything more substantial, you wouldn't tell me. Now, let me get this clear, finally. Your duties in the play never led you to leave the kitchen?"

"Never once. I was there the whole time, even during the Interval, checking costumes and props. Jason aims to give the sense of Jacobean bourgeois life, so in the absence of sets, props are very important."

"And the balcony scene we've mentioned is the only time in the play when the upper stage is used?"

"Yes, the only one."

"I suppose you checked that the room upstairs that led onto the balcony was in fact unlocked?"

"Oh, yes," said Susan unsuspectingly. "But well before the performance started. In any case, Carston had a room key in case one of the maids had locked it by mistake."

Dundy nodded his head and mentally wiped Susan Fanshaw from his list of suspects.

"Of course, I'm onstage practically the whole evening," said Ronnie Wimsett, clearly not immune to the same little vanities as Carston Galloway. "Or just off, or just about to go on. So quite apart from the fact that it would be difficult for me to have done it, it's also difficult for me to remember anything that went on backstage."

"Why? Because if you weren't on, you were hovering about around one of the doors onto the stage?"

"That's right. Whereas someone with a smaller part could certainly spend an hour or more in the kitchen just sitting around and noticing."

Wimsett was a very different type from most of the actors, Dundy decided. Apparently open, genial, conversational, but with an overriding reticence, particularly about himself. On essentials he presented a bland front to the world. Dundy was willing to bet that his fellow actors knew little about his character, his private life, his sexual preferences. He kept, in popular parlance, himself to himself. Like many policemen, Dundy thought.

"Miss Geary ought to be ideal," he said. "She was sitting around for most of the play. But for obvious reasons that she makes no secret of, she's not much use. Tell me, during the weeks of rehearsal, who reacted most strongly to Des Capper?"

"Well..." Ronnie was either plainly reluctant or plainly acting out reluctance. "I suppose you'd have to say Gillian Soames. She'd been *very* fond of Arthur Bradley, the earlier manager, in a father-and-daughter sort of way. I think anyone would have been a letdown. But Capper she thought the absolute pits."

"Yes, she's been quite open about that," said Dundy quickly. The foot of one of his attendant policemen gave a gentle tap on the ankle of the other attendant policeman. "What about the other people staying at the Saracen? How did they react to him?"

"Oh, in various ways. Carston Galloway with a sort of lordly, amused contempt...Clarissa taking the oppor-

tunity for a scene...Connie Geary rather relished him.
She enjoys the chance of plumbing the depths of human
awfulness, and she got that with Des. It's something
actors often enjoy—watching dreadful people, to use
them afterwards." He thought. "I think some of the people whom he most got under the skin of were the ones he
gave advice to." He grinned self-depreciatingly. "That
includes me, I suppose. He tried to educate me in the
method school of acting. He tried to give Krister Kroll a
lesson in breathing techniques, and that riled him."

"Krister Kroll? He is—?"

"The lead tenor in *Adelaide*. He's not staying in the
hotel, but he's been around a fair bit with Peter and
Natalya, having a drink in the Shakespeare, and so on.
He's sung here before, so he knew the Saracen in better
days. He was around after the concert."

"I see. Yes, I saw Mr. Kroll onstage last night. And
what about Gunter Gottlieb?"

"Oh, God! Rather an appropriate exclamation, now
I come to think about it. Gottlieb resembles the God of
our worst fears. Well, I don't think for much of the time
Gottlieb was aware that Des existed. I think that was
probably worse than ridicule as far as Des was concerned. I mean, if we laughed at his ideas of correct
breathing or his cures for the piles, then we were just
wrong, because he'd read it in *All You Want To Know
About Your Innards,* or some such tome, so he *knew.* But
if you just ignored his existence, you undermined his
whole basis for living."

"And Gottlieb did that?"

"I tell you, I once saw him come into the
Shakespeare, where Natalya and Peter Fortnum had been
holed up at a table by Des Capper. Gottlieb wanted to

speak to Natalya—the usual urge to make sure that she did *exactly* as he demanded at some moment of the score, because he has this need for *total* control and a terrible mistrust of anyone else's creative powers. Anyway, instead of asking Des to go away, he just walked over, pushed against his shoulder, and pointed. Des was in full flood about something or other as usual, but he was so astonished he got up, whereupon Gottlieb simply sat down and started in on whatever he wanted to talk about. And all this was done without a word, as if Des were some kind of intrusive insect."

"Yes," said Dundy meditatively. "One sometimes feels in this case that the wrong person got murdered."

"Oh, don't get me wrong," said Ronnie, putting up his hand. "I had no sympathy for Des. He was quite loathsome, but perhaps in ways that are more difficult to convey."

Dundy turned to another aspect. "You mentioned Mr. Fortnum and Natalya Radilova—"

"Ye-es."

"What's going on there?"

"Search me." Ronnie Wimsett shrugged. "They're keeping very quiet about it, whatever it is. I don't think even Gillian knows, and she and Peter are quite close."

"But you agree there's something going on?"

"Seems so. I know that Peter makes long phone calls involving speaking Russian, and German as well, and that he immediately afterwards likes to report back to Natalya. Apparently these calls are to Germany. Make of that what you will."

"Why doesn't she make them herself?" wondered Dundy.

"I'd guess because she only speaks Russian. Peter is

a great linguist. Also she's very involved with rehearsals. She arrived late and has an immensely demanding part, while Peter has quite a small one. I don't imagine it has anything to do with Des Capper's death."

"Except that Des Capper took an interest in it," said Iain Dundy.

When Ronnie had gone, Dundy sat in thought for some moments, then looked at his watch.

"I'm expecting a Russian interpreter at ten-thirty. I wonder if we could call on the hotel for some breakfast? Just tea and toast would keep the inner man happy. And we *are* investigating the death of their manager, however glad most of them seem to have been to see the end of him."

"I'll go and rustle something up," said Charlie, getting up. "They've got a new body from the Beaumont headquarters here today as temporary manager. I'm sure he'll fall over backwards to keep us happy. He'll want us out as soon as possible."

When he had gone, Dundy remained thoughtful. "The difficulty in this case," he said, "is sorting out the wood from the trees. I *think* whatever Fortnum and this Russian lady have been getting up to is undergrowth, to be cleared away. And yet it could be the most important thing that Capper was on to. More important than the Geary woman's drinking, obviously, or the Galloways' sleeping around. The trouble with dealing with arty people is, it's like dealing with foreigners. You don't know what they think is important."

"You mean like a Neapolitan would kill to revenge

his sister's honor, whereas an Englishman wouldn't care tuppence about his?" asked Nettles.

"Aptly put. Though I'm not sure you're entirely up-to-date with Neapolitan mores." Dundy groaned. "I've just thought: This Radilova woman is *both* foreign *and* arty!"

"Right," said Charlie, coming back from the kitchen, a large tray in his hands. "Very sharp, the young man now in charge. Admits he's been sent from the head office to bring things round. Tea, coffee, toast. Something more substantial if we want it; we've only got to ring. *And* a bit of news to go with it."

"News? What's happened?"

"Literally news. On the news headlines at ten, and I happened to hear it in the kitchens. Five musicians have defected from the Moscow Radio Orchestra. They'd just completed the last concert on a short visit to Stuttgart."

"Ah! What happened?" asked Dundy, interested.

"Well, the concert had just ended with a performance of Tchaikovsky's *Wet Dreams* Symphony—Would that be right, do you think?"

"I very much doubt it, but it's a happy thought. Go on."

"Anyway, the conductor and orchestra acknowledged tumultuous applause, and by the time it was over, they found they were five members short: two violins, a cello, and two French horns. Ten minutes later the five were asking for asylum in the nearest police station. There's no doubt they'll get it."

"I suspect," said Dundy, "that this is going to make our task much easier." He looked at Charlie, who was stuffing toast into his mouth. "And now, young Peace, tell us what's on your mind."

"On my mind, sir?"

"On your mind. Come off it. You've been sunk in thought since you got here this morning. Hardly paying attention. Something occurred to you overnight, or maybe at the opera."

"Well…" Charlie stopped eating and looked at Dundy. "It's so fantastic. What's that French word? *Outré.* That's what it is, it's *outré.* Or maybe I just mean sick."

"Come on, man!"

"Well, can I just fetch something from upstairs?" Charlie jumped up and headed for the stairs up to the manager's quarters. A moment later he was back, carrying books. "Look, I'll just put it before you—right? Because if I just explain it, you'll probably think I'm out of my mind. See this book? It was by Des's chair when we first went through the room. It's William Ashbrook's *Donizetti and His Operas,* apparently the standard work borrowed from the local library. Des was wising himself up on the opera, having learned all there was to know about the play. The book was published in 1982. Read what it says about the first version of *Adelaide.*"

He laid the book in front of Dundy, who read it, nodded, and handed it on to Nettles.

"Right. Now here's the program the director gave us last night. Did you read it?"

"Skimmed through it."

"Read the account of the *second* version of the opera, which was only discovered, or put together, a year or so ago."

Dundy read it and looked up at Charlie, a light in his eyes that was the beginnings of comprehension.

"Yes?"

"Now look at this. *Heat and Dust.*"

"Why on earth—?"

"Remember the note in Des's little book? HAD 9? With an arrow pointing to the side. The note *both* belonged on the page about getting Gottlieb *and* referred back to earlier speculations. Look at page nine."

He put the book in front of Dundy. Dundy read it and looked up, aghast.

"I don't believe it."

Charlie stood there silent. He knew that the words meant the opposite of what they said.

"You don't mean—?"

"Maybe that's how Des intended to 'Get Gottlieb," said Charlie.

For a moment there was silence. Then it was interrupted by a knock on the door. The police interpreter had arrived, but he was not really needed. He had met up with Peter and Natalya in the foyer, and both of them were cock-a-hoop, ready to tell all. Peter's exuberance dominated the small manager's office, now decidedly overcrowded.

"Right," he said, rubbing his hands, when they were somehow settled in. "Now we can come clean."

"I suppose it's no good giving you a lecture about how serious an offense it is, misleading a police officer?" asked Dundy.

"No, because this was a once-in-a-lifetime affair, and there was really nothing else we could do. I promise never to do it again and all the things schoolboys promise, but I'm not going to pretend I'm sorry."

"Who precisely is it who's defected?"

"Natalya's father—one of the violinists. And one of the French horns is a young man she's...friendly with. I should say there's no romantic interest between us at all, just so you don't get things wrong."

"Only a very deep friendship," said Natalya in Russian, and in a very Russian way.

"I see. Tell me, was all this cloak-and-dagger stuff necessary? Aren't things much freer, more open, at the moment in Russia?"

Natalya understood that and said something vitriolic in her own language.

"She said, in effect, 'Tell that to the Ministry of Culture,'" put in the interpreter.

"That's it, you see," said Peter. "Glasnost just isn't filtering down. The ministry is run by the same combination of bureaucrats and secret policemen, and they're not changing their ways. Now, Natalya has been allowed abroad before, but there has never been any question of her father being allowed to go at the same time. Natalya has always been adamant in her own mind that she would never defect and leave her father behind. Her mother died young, and they are very close. Her father is with the Moscow Chamber Orchestra, but he deputizes with the Moscow Radio Orchestra when they need a particularly large band or when there is illness. Which there was. Just before coming away on this German tour. Five string players fell ill...I think I should say there may have been a bit of skulduggery, because Natalya somehow hoped her father would be coming before the orchestra even left Moscow."

Peter grinned at Natalya, who smiled mysteriously into her lap.

"Not my business at all," said Dundy.

"I imagine it was something nasty in their vodka at a drinking session," resumed Peter. "Anyway, her father was called on, and for once bureaucracy and the KGB were caught napping: He was allowed out of the country while his daughter was already outside. All this phoning has been to check that he got out, to confirm plans, and so on—all under the guise of innocent-sounding messages from daughter to father. It's as simple as that."

"And these five didn't want to defect until the tour was completed?"

"That's right. The regular members of the orchestra insisted on that. For the honor of the orchestra and so as not to cast a shadow over the whole trip for the others, who would practically have been locked in their hotel rooms. They had a series of concerts in Hamburg, Mannheim, and Frankfurt, then this final one in Stuttgart before flying back. They just got to the end of the *Winter Dreams* Symphony—"

"What an odd name for a symphony," put in Charlie.

"—and *whoosh* they were away. There's no doubt they will be given asylum in Germany. There's so many orchestras there that certainly one or another will want them."

"And Miss Radilova will be joining her father?"

"She hasn't decided where she will live. She's had lots of offers since the concert and last night's *Adelaide*. She's been parrying them with talk of the Ministry of Culture, who normally arrange all this sort of thing, and with a very heavy hand, too. Now she can talk over with Brad Mallory which to accept. A good soprano is never going to starve."

"Was Mr. Mallory in on all this?"

"No."

"That seems odd. He is her agent, isn't he?"

"Yes, but the explanation is simple: He didn't seem to Natalya to be completely reliable. She didn't feel she could trust him not to let something out, say something indiscreet. And I must say I agree with her. So she used me because I could speak German and Russian."

"Right," said Dundy, stirring in his seat. He felt sure that he had now cleared part of the undergrowth away. Was there anything of more vital growth to be revealed? "Well, as far as it goes, that's clear enough. You had no hint that Des Capper was on to all or any of this?"

"No. The phones in the rooms all go through the hotel switchboard, so presumably he could have listened in. Or he could have listened outside my door; he wasn't above doing that. But it was all in German or Russian, and all in coded language, so really I don't think he could have made anything of it. Not anything specific."

"He could have guessed," said Dundy. "It was a fairly obvious possibility."

"Yes, I expect a lot of people wondered," agreed Peter.

"Which brings us," said Dundy, "to what you did on the night of the murder."

Peter Fortnum seemed to lose several degrees of confidence and looked distinctly uneasy.

"Come, come," said Dundy. "You know, I know, everybody knows, that you didn't spend all that time lost in the corridors."

"No," admitted Peter. "Though one can. It wasn't a bad story, and you couldn't have disproved it. Only in fact Connie Geary's room is very close to the main stairwell, so it was comparatively easy to find. I went through the dining room, through the Shakespeare—"

"And Mrs. Capper was there?"

"Oh, yes. Then I went upstairs and fetched the gin...I'd already decided to phone Stuttgart then rather than after the end of the play. Then I could give the news to Natalya as soon as I came off...they put an appalling extra cost on all the calls you make from your rooms here—"

"English hotels are scandalous at that," agreed Dundy.

"—so I went to the pay phone in one of the little alcoves. I am *not* one of the Piccadilly Fortnums, by the way, if they exist, and money is always scarce. That alcove—you can go and look—is a dark little place, and anyone phoning there is not conspicuous. I dialed and then waited while it rang and rang..."

"Yes, go on."

"While I was standing there, someone went past. He didn't see me. He went on—didn't go down the stairs, but went past. You're familiar with the geography up there, are you?"

As familiar as a day or two's acquaintance can make me."

"The first door after the stairwell is the first-floor door to the Cappers' flat. I'm sure it was there that he knocked. It was not more than a few steps after the stairwell, though I couldn't actually see the door."

"Knocked—and went in?"

"Yes. There was a call; then I heard the door open. Then they answered in Stuttgart, and I didn't pay any more attention."

"You haven't told me yet," said Dundy, "who it was who went past."

"No, I know. I wish I didn't have to. I've nothing against him. But it was Brad Mallory."

Dundy looked at Charlie, then down at the books, and in the crowded little room there was silence.

Chapter 15

EN SUITE

When the little office was cleared and the Russian interpreter had gone off to hobnob with Peter and Natalya Radilova in the Shakespeare Bar, the three policemen who were left sat for some moments in thought.

"Brad Mallory is one of the ones I wondered about," said Dundy at last.

"Me, too," said Charlie. "To be honest, there were others, too: I wondered why this American was so often around the Saracen if he loathed Capper's guts. I wondered why Mrs. Capper didn't ring up to the flat to find out what had happened to Des after the Interval..."

"But both those oddities were probably explicable in terms of character," said Dundy. "The tenor is naturally gregarious. Mrs. Capper is a natural doormat."

"Right. But you can't say the same for Brad Mallory. His actions make no sense in terms of character or of anything else. First of all, he leaves the concert halfway through to flap his way to the hotel, and then he expects us to believe that he was so affected by dear Singh's performance that he had to come back to his room to recover himself. The man's an agent, after all!"

"Wouldn't seem to be much future for him in his own profession," commented Nettles.

"Right," agreed Dundy. "There is Singh enjoying a fabulous success, apparently, with critics and opera directors there to hear him—pressured to come by Mallory himself. And we know for a fact—Singh told us—that offers were made to him to work, future engagements, during Interval and later. But what had Mallory done? Sloped off and left Singh to receive all the plaudits and offers of engagements on his own, holding court in the backstage rooms in the Town Hall. What's an agent for if not to take care of things like that?"

"And it wasn't only Singh," chipped in Charlie. "He was also agent, at least in the West, for Natalya Whatsername. She was a great success in the first half, and she was singing again in the second. He didn't even bother to stay and hear her but left her in the lurch, without translator or any sort of intermediary. If she was any ordinary singer in the West, surely she'd have given him the old heave-ho and got herself an agent that didn't go down with palpitations every time his pet protégé sang."

"One other thing," put in Nettles. "He looked in at the Shakespeare on the way up to his room. If he was wanting peace and quiet to recover in, why would he do that? He was looking for someone, and it's a fair bet it was Des Capper."

"It is," agreed Dundy. "Because look at the sequence of events earlier in the evening when he left the Saracen. He'd been in the Shakespeare, and he came out of the main entrance to go to the Town Hall, immediately followed by Des Capper. Now, let's conjecture that precisely then, on the way out of the Shakespeare and through the foyer, Des came up to him—timing it purposely, Mallory being on his way to Singh's triumph—and said something that showed him his secret had been guessed."

Nettles looked ahead of him, hoping to hide the fact that he was not too sure he understood what the secret in question was. Charlie nodded vigorously, knowing all too well.

"That all makes sense," he said with an enthusiasm born of a love of the chase. "But did you get why he thought he could use Mallory and Singh to 'Get Gottlieb'?"

"I think so. I *think* I sorted it out," said Dundy. "Let's get it clear in our minds. Let's go back to that rehearsal we've heard about from more than one witness. It was a rehearsal with full cast and orchestra, but it wasn't a dress rehearsal. I checked that this morning, by the way, with the director. The tenor, Krister Kroll, was in stage costume. That was because he has to wear that rather camp number in furs and tartan. The rest were in mufti."

"I don't get the point," said Nettles. "Remember I haven't seen the show."

"But you read the program. Anyway, as far as I can reconstruct it, this is what happened. The tenor entered at the back of the stage and launched into his big tune. He's got quite a nice voice, but small, and it was quite ineffective—wouldn't have penetrated beyond the third row of the stalls, even I could hear that. So Gottlieb made him come to the front of the stage, and that totally upset the production. Natalya Whatsit got upset, and Brad went up onstage to calm her down, accompanied by Singh— Brad Mallory being the solicitous singers' agent at this point, you notice. How much he could do to calm her down without a common language I don't know, but he certainly tried. Now, at this point Des Capper arrived backstage to assert his right to go everywhere and poke his finger in everything."

"Yes," said Nettles, still puzzled. "He spoke to Peter Fortnum."

"That's right. Then the staging was altered, the scene played through to the end, then a break was called. We needn't go into that. But what would someone arriving at that point in the rehearsal think?"

"That the Third World War was about to start and the Germans were on the other side as usual?" suggested Nettles.

Charlie jumped up and down excitedly. "No! He'd see Singh up there onstage, in civvies like the rest, and he'd assume that he had a part in the opera. Remember that he made that endearing little joke to Fortnum about the Indians running the corner shops?"

"And not only that," insisted Dundy. "Remember that when Fortnum and Gillian Soames first arrived at the Saracen, he thought they were 'the operatic lady and gentleman.' He not only got the wrong people, but he was wrong about Singh, too. He wasn't singing in the opera, only in a concert."

"I still don't quite see—" began Nettles.

"It means," said Charlie, bubbling on, "that if he wanted to get even with Gottlieb, the best way to do it was through the opera—prestige affair, second big event of the festival, the stepping-stone for Gottlieb taking over the festival as a whole. And Des, getting it wrong as usual, thought he could get at the opera via Singh, who he thought was in it."

"What he thought, I'm sure," agreed Dundy, "was that he could bring the whole thing down around

Gottlieb's head by going to the tabloids with a really grubby little story that they'd love. The fact that he'd also destroy Singh's career—and probably Mallory's, too, in the process—wouldn't have worried him. Why would it? He had no reason to love them." He got up and looked at the other two. "Come on. I think it's time that we talked to him."

They got together their things and went out of the office. As they passed the reception desk in the foyer, Iain Dundy pulled out the guest book and found Mallory's rooms. They constituted the Grand Suite—rooms 116 and 117. As they went up the staircase, they threw a glance into the Shakespeare. The new manager, a fair-haired, efficient-looking young man, was coping with the help of Dawn. It was getting on for two, but the bar was very full.

"Ghouls," said Dundy.

Once up on the first floor, the policemen began to have a renewed sympathy with Peter Fortnum's point about the geography of the place. Yes, this *was* a hotel that you wouldn't necessarily get the hang of in a few days. After a few abortive sallies up dead-end corridors and down stunted flights of stairs that led nowhere, they finally came, almost by accident, it seemed, upon room 116. It was next to room 145. Dundy listened outside the door of room 116, then room 117, and finally knocked on the latter door. There was a moment's pause and then a reasonably confident sounding "Come in."

They went in to what was obviously one of the best rooms in the hotel. It was, in fact, a sitting room with bedrooms leading off from either end and a gleaming bathroom visible through a half-open door. In the sitting room there was a large television and radio, a dining table and chairs, and coffee tables dotted here and there. The furniture was either old or new-old, Dundy couldn't decide which. On one of the coffee tables was a tray with plates and glasses on it. Brad and Singh had obviously just lunched on something sent up from the kitchens. Dundy wondered whether Mallory was becoming embarrassed by Singh or fearful for his discovery. A half bottle of German wine stood on the dining table, and beside it a bottle of Coca-Cola.

Singh was sitting in an armchair on one side of a little table, reading *Uomo,* or perhaps just studying the fashion plates. He looked chubby and satisfied, and Dundy thought there might be a suspicion of makeup on his face. Brad Mallory was sitting on the other side, a cravat tucked airily into his open shirt, suede shoes on his feet. In spite of such old-fashioned dash in his attire, it struck Dundy that he looked very small. As he put his book down hurriedly on the table and bustled to welcome them all in, he looked apprehensive, almost frightened. He was not a good dissembler of fear. Dundy bent down and took up the book.

"Ah, press-cuttings," he said. "I hear you had a great success at the concert, sir." Singh, who had watched the bustle as a disinterested observer, allowed his sallow cheeks to crease into a smile but then let them sink back into handsome repose. "I haven't had time to read the reviews myself, but I hear you gave a very remarkable performance."

"The reviews are *very* good, *very* gratifying," said Brad with a nervous, jerky intensity. "It's the beginning of a brilliant career for Singh. But I don't suppose all three of you will have come to talk about music, Superintendent?"

"No, indeed, sir. I wonder if we could speak to you alone? No reason for bothering Mr. Singh in this instance."

Brad Mallory seemed both nervous and yet glad. "Of course, yes. Do you mind, dear boy? The video is in your bedroom. You seem to have been up half the night with it. I'm sure you have something you'd like to play over again."

Singh smiled again and got up gracefully. He moved as if he had studied deportment with some very aged teacher, possibly with Mr. Turveydrop himself. As soon as he had shut the door, the policemen heard a click, then the opening music of *Mary Poppins.*

When he heard it, Brad Mallory flinched, as if this were a masterpiece with which he was all too familiar. Then his face dissolved into a smile.

"The dear boy," he said, looking round at them. "So faithful to his old favorites."

He waved Dundy and the other policemen to seats, but Dundy waited before he accepted.

"The dear boy seems to have pleased the critics as much as he affected you," he said, tapping the collection of pasted-in reviews. "It must be a disadvantage to you in your job to be so easily incapacitated emotionally."

Brad Mallory looked disconcerted. "It *is,* "he said. "But that's one of the penalties one pays for the artistic temperament."

Iain Dundy sat down and gave him a hard look. "Mr. Mallory," he said. "I'm not going to beat about the bush or get into little sparring bouts with you. And I wish you'd drop this performance."

"Performance?"

"It seems to me you're giving a *performance* as an aesthete, practically a parody of one. You remind me of a character in a not very good detective story from the twenties. You also seem to me to be giving a parody performance of a homosexual."

"Like the chaste apprentice in the play," put in Charlie. "He's doing a parody of the *Carry On* homosexual, and you're doing the quivering aesthete one."

"I really don't think you understand the *feelings* of someone who—"

Iain Dundy leaned forward in his chair. "Come off it, old cock. You're a bloody singers' agent. If Singh was such a triumph at the concert the other night, your job was to remain there and talk to the important people you'd invited to hear him. Natalya Radilova was something of a hit, too, and she couldn't rub more than two words of English together. Your job was to stay down there, and you'd have to be a bloody bad agent not to do it. I don't believe you're that. Why did you come away?"

Brad's voice came feebly, hardly penetrating the pepped-up jollities of *Mary Poppins* from the next room.

"I've told you: Singh is something very *special* to me. His singing affected me profoundly."

"Codswallop! If you were that knocked all of a heap emotionally, why did you look in at the Shakespeare before you went up to your room? You were looking for someone. And I may as well tell you that you were seen knocking on Des Capper's door at twenty past eight."

Brad Mallory's jaw dropped, and he gave out a little squawk, like a strangled chicken.

"No! No!"

"Oh, yes. I tell you, you were *seen*. And I've thought all along your story wasn't worth a bean. I think you came back because of something Des Capper said to you as you left the Saracen on your way to the Town Hall."

Again there was this little squawk, and Brad Mallory writhed in his chair as if he were sitting on hot coals. Then quite suddenly he went still, sagging down into the chair like a half-empty sack of potatoes—small, pathetic, tired.

He had dropped the mannerisms, but it was as if the mannerisms had become his self and there was nothing remaining. His eyes stared ahead, the most lively things about him. He was calculating how much he could tell.

"Since you know..." he said in a low voice, hesitating as he chose his revelations with care. "Yes, he did say something to me as I was leaving to go to the concert. He'd already said something loaded in the bar about always meaning what he said. Then when I left he caught up with me in the foyer...I won't say what he said. It's not relevant...By the time I got to the concert, my mind was in turmoil! Absolute turmoil!" He caught Dundy's eye and dropped the mannerism. "I was greeting everyone I knew, everyone I'd asked there, and I was casting around in my mind what I could do. I tried to phone him before the concert started, but there was no answer...He was in the courtyard, watching the play, I believe. I went in for the first half of the concert. Luckily I had an aisle seat at the back. I couldn't settle, couldn't concentrate on anything...During the letter scene, Natalya's aria, just before Singh's pieces, I slipped out and rang him again. This time he was in. I said I had to see him, and at once. I said there was an interval coming up in the concert and that I'd come up to the Saracen at about a quarter or twenty past eight."

"What was his reaction?"

"Very genial...in his dreadful way...Gloating, really. But before he rang off, he said: 'Not that it will do you any good, Mr. Mallory, but I'm quite happy to have a natter about it.'"

"Right," said Dundy, stretching his legs. "Well, that's clear enough so far. Except, of course, that you've skated over the little matter of what Capper was threatening you with."

"It's not rele—"

Dundy held up his hand. There was no reason why Mallory should be allowed to get off this particular hook.

"There's no way this discussion is going to make any sense unless the whole thing is brought into the open. For the moment, this will be among ourselves. What would need to come out at any future trial I can't possibly say as yet. May I suggest that what Des said to you as you were leaving for the Town Hall—"

"*No!* Please, no!"

"—was something like: 'So you're off to see your little castrato performing, are you, Mr. Mallory?'"

Nettles blinked. So that *was* it! The little bundle in the chair, after a brief spasm of life, collapsed again. He looked like Grandmother Smallweed, needing to be shaken up. At last he said:

"Actually what he said was 'Give my best wishes to your pet castrato.'"

"Right," said Dundy, still refusing to let Mallory off the hook. "I'm sure we're all better off for having that out in the open. Now, I think you'd better explain to us all exactly what a castrato was—is—don't you?"

Brad Mallory swallowed and thought. When he spoke, it was very low, as if he were reading to himself from a dictionary of music.

"It was a man who had been castrated just before puberty to preserve his high singing voice. They chose boys with beautiful voices, of course, and as it developed, it became something quite unique—full, brilliant, agile. They used the castrati in the papal choir right up to the end of the nineteenth century, but in opera they more or less died out early in the nineteenth century. The practice had become...unacceptable. The castrati were very spoiled, demanding, capricious, vain, and people got tired of their whims. They also became very fat, so they became ridiculous in heroic parts. But a lot of operas *need* that kind of voice: Handel, Gluck, early Mozart, early Rossini. Nowadays they use women for the parts, or countertenors, but it's not right."

"A countertenor, as I understand it," said Dundy, "is a choirboy who keeps his voice high by a big effort, right?"

"Something like that. The trouble is, the castrato roles call for brilliance and volume, and a countertenor voice is too weak; it won't fill a modem opera house. And a woman's voice is quite different, too, and she always looks like a woman in men's clothes." He cast them a look of feeble cunning. "It's a problem nobody has been able to solve."

"Until you came along," said Dundy quietly. "Until you decided to fill a long-felt want."

Brad Mallory sparked up a little. "It's not as though there weren't any eunuchs around! People talk as if you couldn't do that today. That's just ignorance. It's being done all over the world—Turkey, India..."

"Yes, indeed: India. How did you come to know about the survival of the practice in India?"

Brad Mallory looked down into his lap and again spoke low. "I went there often when we used to arrange a World Theater Festival in London. I was one of the directors. I got to know all the major Indian troupes and some of the lesser—"

"These would have been some of the lesser, wouldn't they?" Dundy shook his head. "This was something that Des Capper also proved to be expert in, wasn't it?"

"Damn the man! Damn the bloody little know-it-all! Yes, I suppose so. We never talked about *how* he came to know. Part of his Indian experiences, presumably."

"Yes, it must have been. Of course, he'd never done most of the things he claimed to have done, but he had been there. This is what I think happened. Des came along to the rehearsal of *Adelaide,* and he happened to come backstage at the moment when you and Singh had gone onstage to comfort or reassure Natalya Radilova. He'd always assumed that Singh was 'an operatic gentleman,' in his words, and this confirmed him in his mistake."

"I can't think what part he imagined he played."

"Ah, but remember that the version of *Adelaide* that is being played here is Donizetti's rewrite from the 1830s, which was only discovered last year. When he went to the standard work on Donizetti, all he found was an account of the *original* opera of 1825, written for the castrato Velluti. So he assumed that Singh was playing Velluti's part of Robert the Bruce. What was actually going on onstage during the bit of rehearsal he saw meant little to him, because it was in Italian, and he hadn't then done a great deal of homework on the opera. He was booking for some way of getting revenge on Gottlieb, particularly later, after the scene in the Green Room. He didn't have much luck with Gottlieb's taste in young girls, because his minder was being careful. So when he got the idea that you had got hold of a *real* castrato for the Velluti part, he got the notion of getting at Gottlieb by turning his operatic triumph into a scandal and disaster that the popular press would seize on like vultures over carrion."

"That's something I don't quite understand, sir," said Nettles. "Would they have been that interested? Opera's pretty much of a minority interest."

"Oh, but they would, they would." Dundy turned to Mallory. "I'm sure you realized that throughout."

Mallory nodded sadly. "Oh, yes. I always knew the public would never stand for a castrated male if they knew. Imagine what the *Daily Grub* would make of the sick tastes of"—his voice took on an Australian twang—"'so-called culture vultures.' Think of the great mountain of pretended outrage and vulgar ridicule they would pile up. They would have a field day. If it were known, Singh could never perform in public again. People would be sickened."

"And Gottlieb's opera would be a disaster. He would be buried in sludge. Except, of course, that unknown to Des Capper, Singh had nothing to do with *Adelaide.* It would have been you who was buried."

"So what we think happened," put in Charlie, "is that Capper saw the rehearsal, went away and read about Donizetti writing the opera for a castrato, and something clicked in his mind, something he remembered from his Indian experiences."

"That's it," resumed Dundy. "India has been in everybody's minds recently, what with *Jewel in the Crown, Gandhi, A Passage to India,* and the rest. No doubt Des bored his saloon-bar regulars with his superior knowledge of the place each time one of them was shown on television. But knowledge he did have, and some reading, too, and when he thought of the subject of eunuchs, he remembered the hijras. He not only remembered them. There was a note in his little book of useful bits of information: HAD 9. He'd remembered that they appeared in *Heat and Dust* and had gone away and looked them up."

"I still don't understand who or what the hijras were," said Nettles. "Or *are.*"

"Are, definitely. Perhaps you could tell him, Mr. Mallory," said Dundy. "I presume it was from them, or through them, that you—what shall we say?—acquired Singh?"

Brad Mallory flinched. His voice was still low, as if he were a great distance away. "They are bands of traveling entertainers. They perform on the streets, at stag parties and suchlike occasions. Probably it would have been at a stag party that Capper saw them. They're hermaphrodites and eunuchs, and their act is scabrous, very sexual, really rather horrible. There is a religious basis somewhere— they have a shrine in Gujarat—but it's not very strong. In fact, for the ordinary Indian they're the next thing to outcasts, though they're very often beautiful, weirdly so, and sometimes talented. Sometimes they buy children; sometimes they kidnap them. Then they castrate them."

"As you knew from your visits to India."

"Yes. I saw a troupe of them the very first time I went there. They fascinated me. They planted a seed in the back of my mind. And when early operas became more and more popular, I thought: *That's* what is needed. Only that sort of voice can really do justice to the music."

"And probably you were right. As we can see from these reviews." Dundy tapped the already pasted in collection of reviews. "They all exclaim how *different* Singh's voice is from the usual countertenor—so much more powerful and brilliant. They guess it's something to do with his being Indian. None of them guesses the real reason. It's interesting that Des Capper did. I wonder what gave him the clue."

"I don't know. I always insisted that Singh was English," said Brad Mallory. "I think I overdid it and gave him the first clue."

"Yes, and I suspect that he was puzzled by your homosexual performance. I suppose you did that to give Singh some kind of sexual identity?"

"Yes. I adopted them gradually, as if I was changing my...my sexual orientation. It was a preparation for when I would bring Singh forward, launch him on his career."

"But I suspect that Des learned from the room maids here that there didn't seem to be anything going on between you. 'Where do they do it?' he asked in his little book...But you haven't told us how you procured Singh."

"If you're suggesting that I had him...*done,* you're mistaken," said Brad with a brief spurt of fire. "He was twelve when I saw him and had already been...operated on. I listened to several of the boys, heard their singing voices, chose the one that seemed most beautiful and most Western. Then I arranged for the boy to be adopted by an Indian couple that I knew in this country. He had no obvious parent or protector, so it was quite easy. From the day he came here he has been having music lessons. Everything has been geared towards his debut...The man who will show us how Handel opera should be sung..."

His voice faded into silence, but then he looked wildly round at the other three men. "I mean, *why not?*" he almost cried.

They didn't tell him. They left a pause, and then Dundy said quietly: "I imagine it hasn't been easy."

Brad Mallory smiled sadly. "Oh, no. It hasn't been

easy. As you've seen, he's very vain and childish. It's almost as if he stopped growing up when...I'm used to artists who view the world as revolving around themselves. That's usual. And they are *artists*. Singh is a baby. At the center there is...a hole. Sweet nothing. And he can be cruel, too. To defenseless things. And he eats sweets..."

"Eats sweets?" asked Nettles, mystified.

"I tell him not to. Already he's getting very chubby. If he becomes grossly fat, he will remind people of nothing so much as the old castrati, and then someone will ask questions. I tell him this over and over, but he takes no notice. He has no gratitude."

"Gratitude?"

"You think he shouldn't have? Maybe. Anyway, he has none. I have this fear that in two or three years, when he has made his name, he will throw me over. All the financial gains will go to someone else. And I'll have nothing to threaten him with to keep him faithful. Any revelation about his...state would tarnish me much more than it would tarnish him. No, it has not been easy."

"I must say I'm rather glad to hear that," said Iain Dundy briskly. "Now, let's come to the night of the murder, sir. Let's hear exactly what happened?"

"Oh, God." Bradford Mallory went white. "It was a nightmare. It needed all my little...queer mannerisms to carry it off...After I'd telephoned, I went back to the Town Hall to hear Singh's arias. He was brilliant, but I could hardly concentrate. What was I going to do? Was I going to offer him money? If so, how much? Was it possible to brazen things out? Because, after all, I didn't see how he could *know.*"

"You left the concert as soon as Singh was finished, did you? When was that?"

"About ten past eight, as I told you before. I was back at the Saracen by a quarter past. I came to this room, put a flannel over my face, lit a cigarette, and put it straight out. It was so *damnable,* after all my work, and just when it was coming to fruition. But I hadn't made up my mind what to do when I went along and knocked at his door. That was about twenty past eight or so, as you said. If only I'd *decided* to face it out or *decided* to pay up. I put up a front, but I think Capper could see from the moment I walked into the room that I was beaten. He behaved as if I was a mouse he'd brought in and was preparing to torment."

"What was he like?"

"Oh—*horrible.* Rubbing his hands with glee, making barroom jokes, leering...He was quite disgusting. I tried to face it out, to say there was nothing to it, but the mere fact that I was there told him that wasn't true. He said a medical examination could prove it one way or another. He said he had a good mate on the *Daily Grub.* I could believe it. It's just the paper Des Capper would know someone from. He said it was the sort of story that paper would love, and he was right there: salacious, voyeuristic, anti-art, and the racial overtones wouldn't have come amiss—they could make something of them. I can just see the headlines. They'd have gloated for days over the sick tastes of opera lovers who could watch a nonman who sang like a woman...All this time he was rubbing his hands and leering and making elephantine innuendos. My God, he deserved to die. I shouldn't say that, but he did."

"What happened next?"

"I offered money, of course. That seemed to delight

him even more. It was me wriggling on the hook. His hook. He positively chortled. It wasn't money he was after, he kept saying. It was to get even. I was quite bewildered. I asked him why he wanted to get even with me. What had I done? Or was it Singh he wanted to get even with? He said he had one or two little scores to settle against both of us, but it was neither, and so there was nothing in the world I could do about it. I just didn't understand. How could revealing Singh's secret get him even with anyone other than Singh or me? He was rubbing his hands and chortling to himself. I just didn't know what to do. It was like being in a maze."

"What *did* you do?"

"What could I? I kept thrashing around in my mind: Could I explain why I'd brought Singh over, trained him? Would he understand? Was there anything he wanted besides money? He was positively gleeful that there was nothing I could do: 'It's a very unfortunate position for you, Mr. Mallory,' he kept saying, 'caught up in a quarrel that's not your own. I'm afraid there's just no way you can prevent me making a splash of it.' He was loving it, of course...Normally I'm quite tough. You're quite right about my little mannerisms; they've become a cover. If you deal with singers all the time, you've got to be tough, believe me. But this situation was beyond me. In the end, with his standing there grinning at me as I wriggled, I just turned and walked out."

There was silence in the room. "Are you telling me that you didn't kill him?" asked Dundy.

Mallory's face was suffused by a hopeless, beseeching expression. "Of course I didn't kill him. I knew there was no chance of your believing me; that's why I didn't even try to tell you part of the story. I knew I probably wouldn't believe it myself if I were in your shoes. But it's the truth. I'm not the killing type."

"When you left the room, he was still alive?"

"Yes!"

"What time was this?"

"About a quarter to nine. The Interval was still on—I remember hearing talking and laughter coming up from the Shakespeare Bar."

"And you never went back to the flat?"

Brad Mallory swallowed. "I went back to the flat. I never went into it."

"What do you mean?"

"I went back to my room. It's just along the corridor, as you know. I lay down on the bed and tried to think. I was desperate for a way out, but there was none. Even in a maze you know there *is* a way out, but now it seemed as though I'd been put down in the middle of one which had had its way out blocked. But—I don't know—perhaps I'm a congenital optimist; perhaps I don't like admitting defeat. I convinced myself I hadn't pushed the money solution hard enough. Perhaps he was just playing with me, I thought, and was really after money all the time. Everyone responds to money, I thought, if you offer enough—and we hadn't even mentioned specific sums. I decided to try again."

"What time was this?"

"Just about nine. I saw the news headlines, downed a quick scotch, and went along that damned corridor again. My hand was just knocking the first knock at Capper's door when it struck me there were low voices inside. And the moment I finished knocking—"

"Yes?"

"I heard a cry—a grunt—and then a heavy thump."

"What did you do?"

"I ran. I knew then that someone had killed him. I ran back to my room and thought over what the hell I should do. For God's sake, I'm not stupid. I knew then that somebody was going to suspect me of murder."

His face was so agonized that it was almost possible to believe him. From Singh's bedroom came the sound of a high soprano voice assuring him that a spoonful of sugar would make the medicine go down.

Chapter 16

THE SHAKESPEARE AGAIN

The last thing Dundy did before he left the suite was caution Brad Mallory not to leave the hotel without getting police permission first. When the three of them were out in the corridor, Charlie noticed a look of dissatisfaction on Dundy's face, a look of niggling doubt. It disappointed him, but he respected the man's greater experience. Dundy walked on but paused at the little dark alcove where the telephone was. There was a sofa there, and an easy chair. Dundy took the latter and sent Nettles to the kitchens for three coffees. Then he took out a cigarette, lit it—the first time Charlie had seen him smoke—and soon began leafing through his notebook. The three of them sipped strong, hot coffee, and all of them kept silent. Charlie was wondering why Dundy was unsatisfied with Mallory as murderer and what were the consequences for the case if his story was believed. Nettles was somehow simultaneously thinking when his wife and new baby would be home and what would be the ideal side for England to field against the West Indies in the first Test. It was a companionable, not a strained, silence. After twenty minutes or so, Dundy's expression of dissatisfaction began to lift.

"You believe him, don't you?" said Charlie.

The disappointment in his voice was palpable. It had been his brilliant deduction that had led them to Mallory, and it should have been crowned by the coup of his arrest.

"I suppose I shouldn't," said Dundy slowly. "We wouldn't have any difficulty in making one hell of a good case against him. All I've got on the other side is instinct."

"Instinct about—?"

"Character, I suppose. I just don't feel he has it in him to commit murder. Oh, I grant you he's tougher than he's been pretending. His job proves that. And the motive is there all right. I believe what he says about Singh's career being ruined is true. It would be destroyed by the popular press. There might be a few recordings, because that's closed-door stuff, but a stage career? I doubt it. I suspect that there is one thing Mallory has lied about. I think it may be that he did "choose" Singh, did pick out the boy with the best voice and the best appearance, and then have him "done." And if that is so, he has a motive whether or not Singh's career would be ruined—because sure as hell *his* would be. The papers would crucify him. So there's no doubt whatever about motive. But guts, courage, bottle, nerve—call it what you will. I don't think he has it to the sort of degree that murder demands. I still think he's basically a gadfly, a dilettante. When he shed all those gay mannerisms, there somehow—how shall I put it?—there wasn't much left. I try to square him with all I've ever learned in my life about killers, and all I've ever read about them, and I can't."

"But where does that leave us, sir?" asked Nettles. "Back at square one?"

"No, of course not," said Dundy crossly. *"Think,* man. Surely you can see that if we believe him it alters our whole perspective on the case."

"Time," said Charlie.

"Exactly."

They all three sat thinking about that for some moments. Downstairs, time had just been called. Dundy stubbed out his second cigarette and got up.

"We'll go down."

In the Shakespeare there were a few stragglers left. Newspapers were strewn around on the tables, mostly turned to the arts pages, and a collection of singers and orchestral players were laughing over an article in the *Times* in which Bernard Levin confessed that he was unable to take Donizetti seriously. At the sight of the policemen, they drank up and left. How they knew they were policemen was no mystery: In the Saracen at the time, it was a fair bet. Dundy noted that among the disappearing party was Krister Kroll, the tenor. He let him go and surveyed the rapidly emptying room with satisfaction. Then he went to the bar, where Dawn and the new temporary manager were tidying up the lunchtime debris.

"Ah, you would be the superintendent," said the new manager, coming round from behind the bar, his manner somewhere between the friendly and the ingratiating. He seemed a pleasant enough young man, but people in any way connected with the licensing trade never quite knew how to behave with policemen.

"That's right," said Dundy. "You've been got here quickly. Getting things round?"

The manager's face assumed a serious expression. "Oh, officially, there's nothing to get round. *Un*officially we may admit that perhaps the best appointment may not have been made last time, that there may be a few bridges to mend."

"I think I might like a brief word, eventually, on how that appointment came to be made."

"Of course. I was briefed about that before I was sent over. Oh, by the way, this came this morning from headquarters." He drew from his pocket a Saracen's Head envelope and handed it to Dundy. "We didn't think there was any need to bother about fingerprints since it had been through the postal mill. It's Capper's handwriting, isn't it? Sent the day he died, but by second-class mail."

There was no letter. What Dundy drew out of the envelope was a newspaper clipping. It was the medical column of one of the newspapers they had found in Capper's flat. It dealt, in laymen's terms, with a newly developed treatment for spastics.

"I think you'll find the appointment quite understandable when you know the facts," the temporary manager was nervously saying. "It's far from suspicious. In fact, redounding to the credit—"

"Right," said Dundy, cutting him short. "But before we go into that—"

"Yes? Anything we can do to help, of course."

"—I'd like to try a little experiment with Dawn here."

Dawn looked up, surprised. She was much more alert today, rested and in almost sparkling form. She had, of course, been very much the center of attention both at home and in the hotel. Now she looked puzzled but intrigued.

"I don't see—"

"You don't have to. It's quite simple, and something you're used to doing. Now, I want you to fill a tray with dirty glasses—or clean ones, if you haven't got enough—just as you did on the night of the murder."

"We do generally prefer to wash them by hand, Superintendent," said the fair-haired manager, then seemed to realize the fatuity of this remark.

"I'm sure you do, sir. You can do them later by hand if you like. Did you load up the tray on your own on the murder night, miss?"

"No, Mrs. Capper helped a bit."

"If you could help her, then, sir?"

As he watched them filling a large tray, which it seemed would be all Dawn could manage to lift or encompass the breadth of in her arms, Dundy was conscious that behind him, at the door into the foyer, there was a movement, a presence. He wondered if it were possible

"Now it's full, isn't it? It's now exactly two-fifty. I want you to take it up, go through with the tray to the kitchens, stack the glasses into the dishwasher just as you did on Thursday, at the same sort of rate you did it then, and then set the machine going, do anything else that you—"

"Oh, my God, you know!"

Win Capper, standing at the doorway, seemed turned to stone, her usually sallow complexion turned to an unhealthy white. Dundy held Dawn back from rushing over to her, and after a minute she tottered forward and sat down on a chair. Dundy released Dawn, who swiftly poured a neat scotch at the bar and hurried over with it. She put it to Win's mouth, then sat beside her at the table and put her arm around her shoulders. Win stared down at the table, then took another gulp at the whiskey.

When she spoke, it was in a dull, flat voice. "I overdid it, didn't I? About how wonderful Des was and how he hadn't an enemy in the world."

"It did occur to me," said Dundy carefully, "that the wife of someone like Des Capper might think he was wonderful, but she couldn't remain unaware that other people didn't share the same view. Not in a pub, where she could see people's reactions to him and would probably overhear opinions of him."

Win nodded. She looked up now, and faint traces of color had begun to come back into her cheeks.

"I'm ready to come along with you. It's almost a relief. I was always afraid someone else was going to be charged. Dawn will help me pack one or two things, won't you, dear? I'd just like to say why I did it"—she patted Dawn's hand—"so you won't think so badly of me."

"I don't," said Dawn, only with an effort refraining from saying that she thought Win had done a public service.

"I expect by now you know what Des was really like. He was mean, cunning, and a slave driver. I should have left him years ago, but perhaps I'm a natural slave. Or I'd become one over the years. I was a nurse when I married him. Guess I just went from slavery to matron to slavery in a bar for Des. Seven years ago I got pregnant. I was over the moon. Des was pretty pleased, too. Me not getting pregnant was one of the things he used to throw in my face the ten years we'd been married. Then Kevin was born, and a few days later they told us he was a spastic…It didn't make any difference to me. I only loved him the more. But that was the end for Des. If he wasn't a healthy, normal child, he just didn't want to know about him. He said you couldn't have an idiot child—that's what he called him—growing up in a pub. The customers wouldn't like it. He had to go into a home. So we put him in one in Lancashire, and I went from Carlisle to see him every Sunday. I didn't think I could ever forgive Des for that, but there was more." She put her handkerchief to her mouth and swallowed.

"The director," murmured the new manager.

"That's right. The director of Beaumont Hotels. He's got a spastic son, too. He brought him to our hotel in Carlisle, on his way to the lake district. He's a wonderful father, devoted, always taking the boy places, bringing him out, arousing his interest. Like I would do if I could see Kevin more than once a week...Of course Des was all over his boy. You'd have thought he was Prince William the way he fawned. And he kept saying it made a *bond*— us having a spastic boy as well. The director was the only person I ever remember Des mentioning him to. And Des said if only we had a bigger hotel to run, with room to bring up a family and to get a bit of privacy—"

"The place in Carlisle is not one of our better hotels," put in the manager. "It's very small and inconvenient, with very little residential trade out of the summer season."

"That's right. Des desperately wanted to get somewhere with a bit of prestige. So he went on and on to the director about how he longed to get Kevin out of the home if only he could get somewhere with a bit of space for him to play, somewhere with a good staff, so I could be freer. After the director went, he used to send him anything he read on cerebral palsy and its treatment. Used to cut things out of papers and the like. Said it was so I shouldn't see them. 'Only set you off again,' he'd say. But he always sent them to the director. When Arthur Bradley died, Des heard about it through the grapevine, of course, and bombarded the director with hints of how he'd like the job and what a difference it would make for Kevin's life…"

"That's true," said the manager. "That's how he got appointed. The director told several people at Head office after we began to get hints that the appointment was not tuning out well. Naturally he felt responsible."

"I won't say I ever believed Des," Win went on, dabbing at her eyes. "But I thought—hoped—that if we got it he'd have to keep his word. I should have known better. We'd been here a month when he wrote to the director and told him Kevin had had a setback and was hospitalized and it would be dangerous to move him…The lying bastard! Kevin was just as he'd always been. But what could I do about it? That's when I decided he had to die. From then on I was just waiting for an opportunity." She got up, now quite steady, and turned to Dawn. "I'll get my things together now, dear, if you'll come with me. It won't take long. Then I'll be quite ready to come with you." She paused at the doorway. "They won't separate me entirely from my boy, will they, sir?"

Dundy hoped he was speaking the truth when he murmured: "No, I'm sure they won't."

As Win and Dawn went up the stairs, Dundy slipped out into the foyer and detailed a police constable to follow them and station himself outside the room. When he got back to the Shakespeare, the new manager had tactfully taken himself off. The others, inevitably, were wanting a bit of a natter.

"I *think* I can see why Brad Mallory's story changed everything," said Nettles, his forehead creased. "We've been going badly wrong over the times, haven't we?"

"Of course we have. Gently led astray by Win Capper. We put so much weight on Des Capper's promise to help at Interval and the fact that he didn't turn up that we began to assume that he was dead by then. But there was nothing in the medical evidence to suggest that he need have been. It was slipshod thinking on my part. Once I'd established that Win must have spent the *first* period when Dawn was away pouring nice cold white wine, I began almost without noticing to exclude her— fool that I was! Because the first person you pay attention to when a husband has been murdered is the wife—and *vice,* of course, *versa.*"

Dundy sat for a moment in thought. "Actually, there were two things of importance in Brad Mallory's story, if we decided to believe it. The first was that Brad rang Des up from the Town Hall to make the appointment for twenty past eight. That meant Des knew well in advance that he wasn't likely to be able to help in the Interval. The second, if we believed him, was that he was *not* dead by Interval—probably not for some time *after* it. That didn't really alter things as far as the play people were concerned, though it let Peter Fortnum off the hook. But it did alter it for others."

"And for Win Capper in particular," said Charlie.

"Yes. I began making an alternative scenario in my mind. You know, people tend to divide murders into premeditated ones and ones done on the spur of the moment. But there is another kind: killings that are *intended* over a long period, the killer merely waiting for a convenient opportunity and then seizing it. That was what we had in this case."

"I think I'm there now," said Charlie. "I think I've got the opportunity Win seized on. Capper rang Win in the bar while Dawn was fetching the snacks."

"That's it, I'm sure. Knowing Des, he might do it,

or he might not. But let's assume he did, at about a quarter past eight, when Dawn was in the kitchen getting the nuts and the cheese dainties. I suspect he did it because he wanted to gloat. He told Win she'd have to cope or get someone else from the kitchen, because he'd be holding someone over a slow fire. He may even have named him. We don't know how much he told Win about his activities and the people he wanted to 'get.' Anyway, she decided then and there that now was the time. As she said, she'd intended doing it for some months, and while the festival people were here was obviously a good time, since Des had put up so many backs. The fact that there was now going to be an interview of murderous potential made this an irresistible opportunity. She was getting ready the drinks for the Interval, which gave her a marvelous alibi for *this* period on her own. As she poured them out, her mind must have been working furiously."

"And she decided not to mention Des's phone call to Dawn when she returned," suggested Nettles.

"That's right. So that when he failed to turn up at Interval, the presumption would be later that he was dead by then. And even if the plan misfired—say, Des came down after his interview with Mallory—well, forgetting a phone call was no great matter. The plan could be put on ice."

"I did wonder," said Charlie, "why she didn't ring up to the flat after the Interval. I thought it must be because she knew he was dead."

"No, it was because she knew that he was alive. So, during the Interval she commented on Des's nonappearance to Dawn, and doubtless within the hearing of customers as well. Then, when Interval was finished, she had to make herself an opportunity. She packed Dawn off with glasses for the big kitchen dishwasher—an unusual procedure but easy to justify. Then she was off through the manager's office, up to the flat. She was just talking to Des—*making* conversation, by the table with the knife on it, perhaps about the problems at Interval—when there was Brad Mallory's knock on the door. Des turned, she took up the knife she'd all along intended as the implement, and she shoved it in his back."

"Come to think of it," said Charlie, "that knife was always a pretty unlikely murder weapon for Brad Mallory."

"Right. It was Indian. It directed too much attention to Singh."

"Another thing," said Charlie. "That damp patch on the cover of the sofa in their flat. It probably came off her apron; she'd been washing up pretty well nonstop all evening."

"Yes. I think she leaned against the sofa to give herself purchase as she stabbed. When I thought about it, there was nobody else, other than Dawn, likely to leave that sort of wet patch."

"And provided she was back in time, she could wash off any blood in the sink in the bar."

"That's it. She went back into the bar, and she acted as usual for the rest of the evening. She wanted the body found as late as possible, of course, so that the *time* of the murder would be reasonably open. So she expressed no great worry about Des's nonappearance, and Dawn, and all the regulars in the bar, knew that Des was just the sort of person who would say he'd turn up and then not do so."

"He hated working in the bar," said Charlie.

"Yes, and it was only his wife who was inconvenienced. He treated her like a skivvy, and he didn't care who knew it. By closing time she thought it would be all right for the body to be found, so she talked to Frank and began to express worry. For a plan that was largely improvised at short notice, it was extremely cunning. It could very well have worked—except that I rather think that if we had charged anybody else, Win would have come forward and confessed. I can't see her letting Brad Mallory take the rap for her."

"Interesting question," said Charlie: "Would we have believed her confession?"

"That's rather a frightening thought," agreed Dundy.

The fair-haired head of the new manager appeared at the dining room door.

"Sorry to intrude. I've just been on the phone to head office. They're glad it's all cleared up, though the fact that it's Mrs. Capper does tie it in rather unpleasantly with the chain. But they've told me to make it plain that they'll do everything in their power in the matter of legal advice, defense, and so on. The director was very insistent on this. Blames himself a lot, as I said before. Feels that if he hadn't pushed for Capper's appointment none of this would have happened. And of course he feels very cut-up about the boy..."

"I can't see the police pushing very strongly for a heavy sentence," said Dundy. "It would be hard to argue that she'd be a danger to anyone else in the future. The courts take a surprisingly lenient view, sometimes, these days, especially in cases of domestic murder."

They heard a sound from the stairs, and the policemen went out into the foyer. Win was coming down the stairs. Dawn was following, carrying a small suitcase.

Win needed no help now. She was quite composed. As Charlie and Nettles went out to usher her from the door to the waiting police car, Dundy went forward to take her arm. She smiled at him, a smile he had not seen before, with some faded prettiness in it.

"I feel much happier now," she said.

Chapter 17

THE WEBSTER

Much later that day, after a long interrogation of Win Capper, the policemen came back to the Saracen. The play was just over, and the audience was streaming out of the great gates or into the three bars. It had been full, of course. If it had not been booked solid before, the murder would have seen to it that it would be now. Rumors that an arrest had been made had rather disappointed most playgoers as they arrived. Secretly many of them had cherished the unlikely hope that at some point in the evening a uniformed cop would stride onstage and arrest somebody, preferably one of the Galloways. Now *that* would be something to tell one's grandchildren!

The policemen collected up their papers and anything they thought might conceivably be used as evidence at the trial. They told the temporary manager that the flat would be available to him in a few days, but he said he didn't fancy it and would use one of the hotel bedrooms. Then there was really nothing more to be done. Yet Charlie and Nettles felt that Dundy was oddly reluctant to be gone. He surely wasn't getting a taste for arty people, was he? Awkwardly they made conversation.

"You'd better be booking your ticket sharpish, hadn't you, sir?" asked Nettles.

"Ticket?"

"For *The Chaste Apprentice.* You'll want to see a performance, won't you, after all we've heard about it?"

"I suppose it might be an idea. I expect they'll let me in if I say I need it to set the seal on my case. As a Ketterick man I can't think why I've never seen a play here before."

"Personally I wish Singh was giving another performance," said Charlie. "Someone might guess the truth at any time, and that will be the end of his career. It would be something to boast about to the sort of girl from London University who fancies a black boyfriend: 'I'm one of the few people in the world who's heard a real castrato.'"

"You have a twisted sense of humor." Dundy's head jerked round. "Oh, I say, excuse me for a moment. Or actually you two can push off home."

But they didn't push off home. They made themselves discreetly scarce and watched while Iain Dundy walked up to Gillian Soames, who had appeared down the stairs from the upper rooms, having changed into civvy clothes. if the superintendent had been a younger man, they would have said that he was chatting her up. It must be said that Dundy got somewhere in a remarkably short time. Indeed, it was almost as if she had been waiting for him to make a move.

"I did wonder if you'd care for a drink," they heard him say after two or three minutes.

Charlie's foot moved for the last time to tap Nettles's ankle.

"I'd love one." Gillian glanced toward the Shakespeare.

"Or even a late supper?" said Dundy, moving towards the street door. "There's a place I know—little Indian place—where they'll still be happy to serve us."

"That would be lovely," said Gillian, following him out into the High Street. "After a performance I always feel I could eat a horse."

Charlie and Nettles looked at each other.

"It has been known," said Nettles. "Policemen marrying actresses."

"Hope for me yet," said Charlie cheerfully.

"Drink?"

"What else?"

"The Shakespeare?"

Charlie looked towards the Shakespeare Bar and seemed to see the ghost of Des Capper leaning familiarly over the shoulders of his guests with his quack remedies, false information, and real threats.

"The Webster," he said firmly.